Oddments

Oddments

A Short Story Collection

Bill Pronzini

Five Star
Unity, Maine

Five Star First Edition Mystery Series.
Published in 2000 in conjunction with Tekno Books
and Ed Gorman.

Set in 11 pt. Plantin by Minnie B. Raven.

Printed in the United States on permanent paper.

Library of Congress Cataloging-in-Publication Data

Pronzini, Bill.
    Oddments : a short story collection / by Bill Pronzini.
       p. cm.
    ISBN 0-7862-2894-6 (hc : alk. paper)
    1. Detective and mystery stories, American. I. Title.
PS3566.R67 O34   2000
813′.54—dc21   00-061029

Table of Contents

The Highbinders

A Carpenter & Quincannon Story

In his twenty years as a detective Quincannon had visited a great many strange and sinister places, but this May night was his first time in an opium den. And not just one—four of them, so far. Four too many.

Blind Annie's Cellar, this one was called. Another of the reputed three hundred such resorts that infested the dark heart of San Francisco's Chinatown. Located in Ross Alley, it was a foul-smelling cave full of scurrying cats and yellowish-blue smoke that hung in ribbons and layers. The smoke seemed to move lumpily, limp at the ends; its thick-sweet odor, not unlike that of burning orange peel, turned Quincannon's seldom-tender stomach for the fourth straight time.

"The gentleman want to smoke?"

The question came in a scratchy singsong from a rag-encased crone seated on a mat just inside the door. On her lap was a tray laden with nickels—the price of admittance. Quincannon said, "No, I'm looking for someone," and added a coin to the litter on the tray. The old woman nodded and grinned, revealing toothless gums. It was a statement, he thought sourly, she had heard a hundred times before. Blind Annie's, like the other three he'd entered, was a democratic resort that catered to Caucasian "dude fiends"—well-dressed ladies and diamond-studded gentlemen—as well as to Chi-

7

nese coolies with twenty-cent *yenshee* habits. Concerned friends and relatives would come looking whenever one of these casual, and in many cases not so casual, hop-smokers failed to return at an appointed time.

Quincannon moved deeper into the lamp-streaked gloom. Tiers of bunks lined both walls, each outfitted with nut-oil lamp, needle, pipe, bowl, and supply of *ah pin yin*. All of the bunks in the nearest tier were occupied. Most smokers lay still, carried to sticky slumber by the black stuff in their pipes. Only one was Caucasian, a man who lay propped on one elbow, smiling fatuously as he held a lichee-nut shell of opium over the flame of his lamp. It made a spluttering, hissing noise as it cooked. Quincannon stepped close enough to determine that the man wasn't James Scarlett, then turned toward the far side of the den.

And there, finally, he found his quarry.

The young attorney lay motionless on one of the lower bunks at the rear, his lips shaping words as if he were chanting some song to himself. Quincannon shook him, slapped his face. No response. Scarlett was a serious addict; he regularly "swallowed a cloud and puffed out fog," as the Chinese said, and escaped for hours, sometimes days, deep inside his pipe dreams.

"You're a blasted fool, all right," Quincannon told the deaf ears. "This is the last section of the city you should've ventured into on this night. It's a wonder you're not dead already." He took a grip on the attorney's rumpled frock coat, hauled him around and off the bunk. There was no protest as he hoisted the slender body over his shoulder.

He was halfway to the door with his burden when his foot struck one of the darting cats. It yowled and clawed at his leg, pitching him off balance. He reeled, cursing, against one of the bunks, dislodged a lamp from its edge; the glass chimney shattered on impact, splashing oil and wick onto the filthy floor matting. The flame that sprouted was thin, shaky; the lack of oxygen in the room kept it from flaring high and spreading. Quincannon stamped out the meager fire and then strained over at the waist, righted the lamp with his free hand. When he stood straight again he heard someone giggle, someone else begin to sing in a low tone. None of the pipers whose eyes were still open paid him the slightest attention. Neither did the smiling crone by the door.

He shifted Scarlett's inert weight on his shoulder. "Opium fiends, tong rivalry, body snatching," he muttered as he staggered past the hag. "Bah, what a case!"

Outside he paused to breathe deeply several times. The cold night air cleared his lungs of the *ah pin yin* smoke and restored his equilibrium. It also roused Scarlett somewhat from his stupor. He stirred, mumbled incoherent words, but his body remained flaccid in Quincannon's grasp.

Nearby, a streetlamp cast a feeble puddle of light; farther down Ross Alley, toward Jackson Street where the hired buggy and driver waited, a few strings of paper lanterns and the glowing brazier of a lone sidewalk food seller opened small holes in the darkness. It was late enough, nearing midnight, so that few pedestrians were abroad. Not many law-abiding Chinese ventured out at this hour. Nor had in the past fifteen years, since the rise of the murderous tongs in the early 'eighties. The Quarter's nights belonged to the hop-smokers and fan-tan gamblers, the slave-girl prostitutes ludicrously called "flower willows," and the *boo how doy*, the tongs' paid hatchet men.

Quincannon carried his burden toward Jackson, his footsteps echoing on the rough cobbles. James Scarlett mumbled again, close enough to Quincannon's ear and with enough lucidity for the words—and the low, fearful tone in which he uttered them—to be distinguishable.

"Fowler Alley," he said.

"What's that, my lad?"

A moan. Then something that might have been "blue shadow."

"Not out here tonight," Quincannon grumbled. "They're all black as the devil's fundament."

Ahead he saw the buggy's driver hunched fretfully on the seat, one hand holding the horse's reins and the other tucked inside his coat, doubtless resting on the handle of a revolver. Quincannon had had to pay him handsomely for this night's work—too handsomely to suit his thrifty Scots nature, even though he would see to it that Mrs. James Scarlett paid the expense. If it had not been for the fact that highbinders almost never preyed on Caucasians, even a pile of greenbacks wouldn't have been enough to bring the driver into Chinatown at midnight.

Twenty feet from the corner, Quincannon passed the lone food seller huddled over his brazier. He glanced at the man, noted the black coolie blouse with its drooping sleeves, the long queue, the head bent and shadow-hidden beneath a black slouch hat surmounted by a red topknot. He shifted his gaze to the buggy again, took two more steps

Coolie food sellers don't wear slouch hats . . . one of the badges of the highbinder . . .

The sudden thought caused him to break stride and turn awkwardly under Scarlett's weight, his hand groping beneath his coat for the holstered Navy Colt. The Chinese was already on his feet. From inside one sleeve he had drawn a long-barreled revolver; he aimed and fired before Quincannon could free his weapon.

The bullet struck the limp form of James Scarlett, made it jerk and slide free. The gunman fired twice more, loud reports in the close confines of the alley, but Quincannon was already falling sideways, his feet torn from under him by the attorney's toppling weight. Both slugs missed in the darkness, one singing in ricochet off the cobbles.

Quincannon struggled out from under the tangle of Scarlett's arms and legs. As he lurched to one knee he heard the retreating thud of the highbinder's footfalls. Heard, too, the rattle and slap of harness leather and bit chains, the staccato beat of horse's hooves as the buggy driver whipped out of harm's way. The gunman was a dim figure racing diagonally across Jackson. By the time Quincannon gained his feet, the man had vanished into the black maw of Ragpickers' Alley.

Fury drove Quincannon into giving chase even though he knew it was futile. Other narrow passages opened off Ragpickers'—Bull Run, Butchers' Alley with its clotted smells of poultry and fish. It was a maze made for the *boo how doy;* if he tried to navigate it in the dark, he was liable to become lost—or worse, leave himself wide open for ambush. The wisdom of this finally cooled his blood, slowed him to a halt ten rods into the lightless alleyway. He stood listening, breathing through his mouth. He could still hear the assassin's footfalls, but they were directionless now, fading. Seconds later, they were gone.

Quickly he returned to Jackson Street. The thoroughfare was empty, the driver and his rig long away. Ross Alley appeared deserted, too, but he could feel eyes peering at him from behind curtains and glass. The highbinder's brazier still burned; in its orange glow James Scarlett was a motionless bulk on the cobbles where he'd fallen. Quincannon went to one knee, probed with fingers that grew wet with blood. One bullet had entered the middle of the attorney's back, shattering the spine and no doubt killing him instantly.

If the Kwong Dock tong was responsible for this, Quincannon thought grimly, war between them and the Hip Sing could erupt at any time. The theft of Bing Ah Kee's corpse was bad enough, but the murder of a Hip Sing shyster—and a white man at that—was worse because of the strong threat of retaliation by police raiders and mobs of Barbary Coast and Tar-Flat toughs. All of Chinatown, in short, was a power keg with a lighted fuse.

The Hall of Justice, an imposing gray stone pile at Kearney and Washington streets, was within stampeding distance of the Chinese Quarter. Quincannon had never felt comfortable inside the building. For one thing, he'd had a run-in or two with the city's constabulary, who did not care to have their thunder stolen by a private investigator who was better at their job than they were. For another thing, police corruption had grown rampant in recent times. Just last year there had been a departmental shakeup in which several officers and Police Clerk William E. Hall were discharged. Chief Crowley claimed all the bad apples had been removed and the barrel was now clean, but Quincannon remained skeptical.

He hid his edginess from the other three men present in the chief's office by carefully loading and lighting his favorite briar. One of the men he knew well enough, even grudgingly respected; this was Lieutenant William Price, head of the Chinatown "flying squad" that had been formed in an effort to control tong crime. He had mixed feelings about Crowley, and liked Sergeant Adam Gentry, Price's assistant, not at all. Gentry was contentious and made no bones about his distaste for flycops.

Short and wiry, a rooster of a man in his gold-buttoned uniform, Gentry watched with a flinty gaze as Quincannon shook out the sulphur match. "Little Pete's behind this, sure as hell. No one else in Chinatown would have the audacity to order the shooting of a white man."

"So it would seem," Quincannon allowed.

"Seem? That bloody devil controls every tong in the Quarter except the Hip Sing."

This was an exaggeration. Fong Ching, alias F.C. Peters, alias Little Pete, was a powerful man, no question—a curious mix of East and West, honest and crooked. He ran several successful businesses, participated in both Chinatown and city politics, and was cultured enough to write Chinese stage operas, yet he ruled much of Chinatown crime with such cleverness that he had never been prosecuted. But his power was limited to a few sin-and-vice tongs. Most tongs were law-abiding, self-governing, and benevolent.

Quincannon said, "The Hip Sing is Pete's strongest rival, I'll grant you that."

"Yes, and he's not above starting a bloodbath in China-town to gain control of it. He's a menace to white and yellow alike."

"Not so bad as that," Price said. "He already controls the blackmail, extortion, and slave-girl rackets, and the Hip Sing is no threat to him there. Gambling is their game, and under Bing Ah Kee there was never any serious trouble between them. That won't change much under the new president, Mock Don Yuen, though it could if that sneaky son of his, Mock Quan, ever takes over."

"Pete's power-mad," Gentry argued. "He wants the whole of Chinatown in his pocket."

"But he's not crazy. He might order the snatching of Bing's remains—though even the Hip Sing aren't convinced he's behind that business or there'd have been war declared already—but I can't see him risking the public execution of a white man, not for any reason. He knows it'd bring us down on him and his highbinders with a vengeance. He's too smart by half to allow that to happen."

"I say he's not. There's not another man in that rat-hole of vice who'd dare to do it."

Quincannon said, "Hidden forces at work, mayhap?"

"Not bloody likely."

"No, it's possible," Price said. He ran a forefinger across his thick moustache. He was a big man, imposing in both bulk and countenance; he had a deserved reputation in Chinatown as the "American Terror," the result of raiding parties he'd led into the Quarter's dens of sin. "I've had a feeling that there's more than meets the eye and ear in Chinatown these days. Yet we've learned nothing to corroborate it."

"Well, I don't care which way the wind is blowing over there," the chief said. "I don't like this damned shooting tonight." Crowley was an overweight sixty, florid and pompous. Politics was his game; his policeman's instincts were suspect, a failing which sometimes led him to rash judgment and action. "The *boo how doy* have always left Caucasians strictly alone. Scarlett's murder sets a deadly precedent and I'm not going to stand by and do nothing about it."

Gentry had lighted a cigar; he waved it for emphasis as he said, "Bully! Finish off Little Pete and his gang before he has more innocent citizens murdered, that's what I say."

"James Scarlett wasn't innocent," Price reminded him. "He sold his soul to the Hip Sing for opium, defended their hatchet men in court. And he had guilty knowledge of the theft of Bing's corpse, possibly even a hand in the deed, according to what Quincannon has told us."

"According to what Scarlett's wife told my partner and me," Quincannon corrected, "though she said nothing of an actual involvement in the body snatching. Only that he had knowledge of the crime and was in mortal fear of his life. Whatever he knew, he kept it to himself. He never spoke of

Little Pete or the Kwong Dock to Mrs. Scarlett."

"They're guilty as sin, just the same," Gentry said. "By God, the only way to ensure public safety is to send the flying squad out to the tong headquarters and Pete's hangouts. Axes, hammers, and pistols will write their epitaphs in a hurry."

"Not yet," Price said. "Not without proof."

"Well, then, why don't we take the squad and find some? Evidence that Pete's behind the killing. Evidence to point to the cold storage where old Bing's bones are stashed."

"Pete's too clever to leave evidence for us to find."

"He is, but maybe his highbinders aren't."

"The sergeant has a good point," Chief Crowley said. "Will, take half a dozen men and go over those places with a fine-tooth comb. And don't take any guff from Pete and his highbinders while you're about it."

"Just as you say, Chief." Price turned to his assistant. "Round up an interpreter and assemble the men we'll need."

"Right away." Gentry hurried from the office.

Quincannon asked through a cloud of pipe smoke, "What do you know of Fowler Alley, Lieutenant?"

"Fowler Alley? Why do you ask that?"

"Scarlett mumbled the name after I carried him out of Blind Annie's. I wonder if it might have significance."

"I can't imagine how. Little Pete hangs out at his shoe factory on Bartlett Alley and Bartlett is where the Kwong Dock Company is located, too. I know there are no tongs headquartered in Fowler Alley. And no illegal activity."

"Are any of the businesses there run by Pete?"

"Not to my knowledge. I'll look into it."

Quincannon nodded, thinking: Not before I do, I'll wager. He got to his feet. "I'll be going now, if you've no objection."

Chief Crowley waved a hand. "We'll notify you if you're needed again."

"Will you bring Mrs. Scarlett word of her husband's death?"

"I'll dispatch a man." The Chief added wryly, "I imagine she'd rather not hear it from you, under the circumstances."

Quincannon said, "I expect not," between his teeth and took his leave.

The law offices of James Scarlett were on the southern fringe of Chinatown, less than half a mile from the Hall of Justice. Quincannon had visited the dingy, two-story building earlier in the day, after leaving Andrea Scarlett with Sabina. The place had been dark and locked up tight then; the same was true when he arrived there a few minutes past midnight.

He paid the hansom driver at the corner, walked back through heavy shadows to the entranceway. Brooding the while, as he had in the cab, about the incident in Ross Alley. How had the gunman known enough to lie in ambush as he had? If he'd been following Scarlett, why not simply enter the opium resort and shoot him there? Witnesses were never a worry to highbinders. The other explanation was that it was Quincannon who had been followed, though it seemed impossible that anyone in Chinatown could know that Carpenter and Quincannon, Professional Detective Services, had been hired by Mrs. Scarlett to find and protect her husband.

Then there was the fact that the assassin had fired three shots, the last two of which had come perilously close to sending Quincannon to join *his* ancestors. Poor and hurried shooting caused by darkness? Or had he also been a target? Something about the gunman fretted him, too, something he could not quite put his finger on.

The whole business smacked of hidden motives, for a fact.

And hidden dangers. He did not like to be made a pawn in any piece of intrigue. He liked it almost as little as being shot at, intentionally or otherwise, and failing at a job he had been retained to do. He meant to get to the bottom of it, with or without official sanction.

Few door latches had ever withstood his ministrations, and the one on James Scarlett's building was no exception. Another attorney occupied the downstairs rooms; Quincannon climbed a creaky staircase to the second floor. The pebbled-glass door imprinted with the words *J. H. Scarlett, Attorney-at-Law* was not locked. This puzzled him slightly, though not for long.

Inside, he struck a sulphur match, found the gas outlet—the building was too old and shabby to have been wired for electricity—and lit the flame. Its pale glow showed him a dusty anteroom containing two desks whose bare surfaces indicated that it had been some while since they had been occupied by either law clerk or secretary. He proceeded through a doorway into Scarlett's private sanctum.

His first impression was that the lawyer had been a remarkably untidy individual. A few seconds later he revised this opinion; the office had been searched in a hurried but rather thorough fashion. Papers littered the top of a large oak desk, the floor around it, and the floor under a bank of wooden file cases. Two of the file drawers were partly open. A wastebasket behind the desk had been overturned and its contents gone through. A shelf of law books showed signs of having been examined as well.

The fine hand of a highbinder? Possibly, though the methods used here were a good deal less destructive than those usually employed by the *boo how doy*.

The smell of must and mildew wrinkled his nostrils as he crossed to the desk, giving him to wonder just how much time

17

Scarlett had spent in these premises. The office wanted a good airing, if not a match to purge it completely. Scowling, he sifted through the papers on and below the desk. They told him nothing except that almost all of Scarlett's recent clients had been Chinese; none of the names was familiar and none of the addresses was on Fowler Alley. The desk drawers yielded even less of interest, and the slim accumulation of briefs, letters, and invoices in the file drawers was likewise unproductive. None bore any direct reference to either the Hip Sing or Kwong Dock tongs, or to Fong Ching under his own name or any of his known aliases.

The only interesting thing about the late Mr. Scarlett's office, in fact, was the state in which Quincannon had found it. What had the previous intruder been searching for? And whatever it was, had he found it?

Sabina was already at her desk when he arrived at the Market Street offices of Carpenter and Quincannon, Professional Detective Services, at nine A.M. She looked bright and well-scrubbed, her glossy black hair piled high on her head and fastened with a jade barrette. As always, Quincannon's hard heart softened and his pulses quickened at sight of her. A fine figure of a woman, Mrs. Sabina Carpenter. For a few seconds, as he shed his derby but not his Chesterfield, the wicked side of his imagination speculated once again on what that fine figure would look like divested of its skirt and jacket, shirtwaist and lacy undergarments. . . .

She narrowed her eyes at him as he crossed the room. "Before we get down to business," she said, "I'll thank you to put my clothes back on."

"Eh?" Sudden warmth crept out of Quincannon's collar. "My dear Sabina! You can't think that I—"

"I don't think it, I know it. I know *you*, John Quincannon,

18

far better than you think I do."

He sighed. "Perhaps, though you often mistake my motives."

"I doubt that. Was your sleepless night a reward of that lascivious mind of yours?"

"How did you know—"

"Bloodshot eyes in saggy pouches. If I didn't know better, I'd think you had forsaken your temperance pledge."

"Observant wench. No, it was neither Demon Rum nor impure thoughts nor my misunderstood affections for you that kept me awake most of the blasted night."

"What, then?"

"The death of James Scarlett and the near death of your most obedient servant."

The words startled her, though only someone who knew Sabina as he did would have been aware of it; her round face betrayed only the barest shadow of her surprise. "What happened, John?"

He told her in detail, including the things that bothered him about the incident and the speculations shared with the three police officers. The smooth skin of her forehead and around her generous mouth bore lines of concern when he finished.

"Bad business," she said. "And bad for business, losing a man we were hired to protect to an assassin's bullet. Not that you're to be blamed, of course."

"Of course," Quincannon said sardonically. "But others will blame me. The only way to undo the damage is for me to find the scoundrel responsible before the police do."

"Us to find him, you mean."

"Us," he agreed.

"I suppose it's back to Chinatown for you."

"It's where the whole of the answer lies."

"Fowler Alley?"

"If Scarlett's mutterings were significant and not part of a hop dream."

"You said he sounded frightened when he spoke the name. Opium dreams are seldom nightmares, John. Men and women use the stuff to escape *from* nightmares, real or imaginary."

"True."

"Scarlett's other words—'blue shadow.' A connection of some sort to Fowler Alley?"

"Possibly. I'm not sure but what I misheard him and the phrase only sounded like 'blue shadow.'"

"Spoken in the same frightened tone?"

Quincannon cudgeled his memory. "I can't be certain."

"Well, our client may have some idea. While you're in Chinatown, I'll pay a call on her."

"I was about to suggest that." He didn't add that this was a task he himself wished to avoid at all costs. Facing a female client whom he had failed would have embarrassed him mightily. The job required Sabina's fine, tactful hand. "Ask her if she knows of any incriminating documents her husband might have had in his possession. And where he kept his private papers. If it wasn't at his office, the mug who searched it before me may not have found what he was after."

"I will. Who would the mug be, do you suppose, if not one of Little Pete's highbinders?"

"I don't say that it wasn't a highbinder. Only that the job seemed to have a more professional touch than the hatchet man's usual ham-fisted tactics."

"Is there anything you can remember about the gunman?" Sabina asked. "It's possible he was known to Mrs. Scarlett as well as her husband."

"It was too dark and his hat pulled too low for a clear squint at his face. Average size, average height." Quincannon scratched irritably at his freebooter's whiskers. "Still, there was something odd about him. . . ."

"Appearance? Movements? Did he say anything?"

"Not a word. Hell and damn! I can't seem to dredge the thing up."

"Let it be and it'll come to you eventually."

"Eventually may be too late." Quincannon clamped his derby on his head, squarely, the way he always wore it when he was on an important mission. "Enough talk. It's action I crave and action I'll have."

"Not too much of it, I hope. Shall we meet back here at one o'clock?"

"If I'm not here by then," Quincannon said, "it'll be because I'm somewhere with my hands around a highbinder's throat."

Fowler Alley was a typical Chinatown passage: narrow, crooked, packed with men and women mostly dressed in the black clothing of the lower-caste Chinese. Paper lanterns strung along rickety balconies and the glowing braziers of food sellers added the only color and light to a tunnel-like expanse made even more gloomy by an overcast sky.

Quincannon, one of the few Caucasians among the throng, wandered along looking at storefronts and the upper floors of sagging firetraps roofed in tarpaper and gravel. Many of the second and third floors were private apartments, hidden from view behind dusty, curtained windows. Some of the business establishments were identifiable from their displayed wares: restaurants, herb shops, a clothiers, a vegetable market. Others, tucked away behind closed doors, darkened windows, and signs in inexplicable Chinese characters, remained a mystery.

Nothing in the alley aroused his suspicions or pricked his

curiosity. There were no tong headquarters here, no opium resorts or fan-tan parlors or houses of ill repute; and nothing even remotely suggestive of blue shadows.

Quincannon retraced his steps through the passage, stopping the one other white man he saw and several Chinese. Did anyone know James Scarlett? The Caucasian was a dry-goods drummer on his second and what he obviously hoped would be his last visit to the Quarter; he had never heard of Scarlett, he said. All the Chinese either didn't speak English or pretended they didn't.

Fowler Alley lay open on both ends, debouching into other passages, but at least for the present, Quincannon thought sourly as he left it, it was a dead end.

The Hip Sing tong was headquartered on Waverly Place, once called Pike Street, one of Chinatown's more notorious thoroughfares. Here, temples and fraternal buildings stood cheek by jowl with opium and gambling dens and the cribs of the flower willows. Last night, when Quincannon had started his hunt for James Scarlett, the passage had been mostly empty; by daylight it teemed with carts, wagons, buggies, half-starved dogs and cats, and human pedestrians. The noise level was high and constant, a shrill tide dominated by the lilting dialects of Canton, Shanghai, and the provinces of Old China.

Two doors down from the three-story tong building was the Four Families Temple, a building of equal height but a much more ornate facade, its balconies carved and painted and decorated with pagoda cornices. On impulse Quincannon turned in through the entrance doors and proceeded to what was known as the Hall of Sorrows, where funeral services were conducted and the bodies of the high-born were laid out in their caskets for viewing. Candlelight flickered; the pungent odor of incense assailed him. The long room, deserted at the moment, was ceiled with a massive scrolled wood carving covered in gold leaf, from which hung dozens of lanterns in pink and green, red and gold. At the far end were a pair of altars with a red prayer bench fronting one. Smaller altars on either side wore embroidered cloths on which fruit, flowers, candles, and joss urns had been arranged.

It was from here that the remains of Bing Ah Kee, venerable president of the Hip Sing Company, had disappeared two nights ago. The old man had died of natural causes and his corpse, after having been honored with a lavish funeral parade, had been returned to the temple for one last night; the next morning it was scheduled to be placed in storage to await passage to Bing's ancestral home in Canton for burial. The thieves had removed the body from its coffin and made off with it sometime during the early morning hours—a particularly bold deed considering the close proximity of the Hip Sing building. Yet they had managed it unseen and unheard, leaving no clue as to their identity or purpose.

Body snatching was uncommon but not unheard of in Chinatown. When such ghoulishness did occur, tong rivalry was almost always the motivating factor—a fact which supported Sergeant Gentry's contention that the disappearance of Bing Ah Kee's husk was the work of Little Pete and the Kwong Dock. Yet stealing an enemy leader's bones without openly claiming responsibility was a damned odd way of warmongering. The usual ploy was a series of assassinations of key figures in the rival tong by local or imported hatchet men.

Why, then, if Little Pete wanted all-out warfare with the Hip Sing, would he order the murder of a white attorney to shut his mouth, but not also order the deaths of Hip Sing highbinders and elders?

The odor of fish was strong in Quincannon's nostrils as he

left the temple. And the stench did not come from the fish market on the opposite side of the street.

The ground floor of the Hip Sing Company was a fraternal gathering place, open to the street; the two upper floors, where tong business was conducted, were closed off and would be well guarded. Quincannon entered freely, passed down a corridor into a large common room. Several black-garbed men, most of them elderly, were playing mah-jongg at a table at one end. Other men sat on cushions and benches, sipping tea, smoking, reading newspapers. A few cast wary glances at the *fan kwei* intruder, but most ignored him.

A middle-aged fellow, his skull completely bald except for a long, braided queue, approached him, bowed, and asked in halting English, "There is something the gentleman seeks?"

Quincannon said, "An audience with Mock Don Yuen," and handed over one of his business cards.

"Please to wait here, honorable sir." The Chinese bowed again, took the card away through a doorway covered by a worn silk tapestry.

Quincannon waited. No one paid him the slightest attention now. He was loading his pipe when the bald man returned and said, "You will follow me, please."

They passed through the tapestried doorway, up a stairway so narrow Quincannon had to turn his body slightly as he ascended. Another man waited at the top, this one young, thickset, with a curved scar under one eye and both hands hidden inside the voluminous sleeves of his blouse. Highbinder on guard duty: those sleeves would conceal revolver or knife or short, sharp hatchet, or possibly all three.

As the bald one retreated down the stairs, highbinder and "foreign devil" eyed one another impassively. Quincannon had no intention of relinquishing his Navy Colt; if any effort were made to search him, he would draw the weapon and take his chances. But the guard made no such attempt. In swift, gliding movements he turned and went sideways along a hallway, his gaze on Quincannon the whole while. At an open doorway at the far end, he stopped and stood as if at attention. When Quincannon entered the room beyond, the highbinder filled the doorway behind him as effectively as any panel of wood.

The chamber might have been an office in any building in San Francisco. There was a long, high desk, a safe, stools, round table set with a tea service. The only Oriental touches were a red silk wall tapestry embroidered with threads of gold, a statue of Buddha, and an incense bowl that emitted a rich, spicy scent. Lamplight highlighted the face of the man standing behind the desk—a man of no more than thirty, slender, clean-shaven, his hair worn long but unqueued, western-style, his body encased in a robe of red brocaded silk that didn't quite conceal the shirt and string tie underneath. On one corner of the desk lay a black slouch hat with a red topknot. Quincannon said, "You're not Mock Don Yuen."

"No, I am Mock Quan, his son."

"I asked for an audience with your father."

"My father is not here, Mr. Quincannon." Mock Quan's English was unaccented and precise. "I have been expecting you."

"Have you now."

"Your reputation is such that I knew you would come to ask questions about the unfortunate occurrence last night."

"Questions which you'll answer truthfully, of course."

"Truth is supreme in the house of Hip Sing."

"And what is the truth of James Scarlett's death?"

"It was arranged by the Kwong Dock and their cowardly leader, Fong Ching. You must know this."

Quincannon shrugged. "For what purpose?"

"Fong is vicious and unscrupulous and his hunger for power has never been sated. He hates and fears the Hip Sing, for we are stronger than any of the tongs under his yoke. He wishes to destroy the Hip Sing so he may reign as king of Chinatown."

"He's the king now, isn't he?"

"No!" Mock Quan's anger came like the sudden flare of a match. Almost as quickly it was extinguished, but not before Quincannon had a glimpse beneath the erudite mask. "He is a fat jackal in lion's skin, the son of a turtle."

That last revealed the depth of Mock Quan's loathing for Little Pete; it was the bitterest of Chinese insults. Quincannon said, "Jackals feed on the dead. The dead such as Bing Ah Kee?"

"Oh yes, it is beyond question Fong Ching is responsible for that outrage as well."

"What do you suppose was done with the body?"

Mock Quan made a slicing gesture with one slim hand. "Should the vessel of the honorable Bing Ah Kee have been destroyed, may Fong Ching suffer the death of a thousand cuts ten thousand times through eternity."

"If the Hip Sing is so sure he's responsible, why has nothing been done to retaliate?"

"Without proof of Fong Ching's treachery, the decision of the council of elders was that the wisest course was to withhold a declaration of war."

"Even after what happened to James Scarlett? His murder could be termed an act of open aggression."

"Mr. Scarlett was neither Chinese nor a member of the Hip Sing Company, merely an employee." Mock Quan took a pre-rolled cigarette from a box on his desk, fitted it into a carved ivory holder. "The council met again this morning. It was decided then to permit the American Terror, Lieutenant Price, and his raiders to punish Fong Ching and the Kwong Dock, thus to avoid the shedding of Hip Sing blood. This will be done soon."

"What makes you so sure?"

"The police now have evidence of Fong Ching's guilt."

"Evidence?" Quincannon scowled. "What evidence?"

"The Kwong Dock highbinder who shot Mr. Scarlett was himself shot and killed early this morning, during a police raid on Fong Ching's shoe factory. A letter was found on the *kwei chan* bearing the letterhead and signature of the esteemed attorney."

"What kind of letter?"

"I do not know," Mock Quan said. "I know only that the American Terror is preparing to lead other raids which will crush the life from the turtle's offspring."

Quincannon was silent for a time, while he digested this new information. If anything, it deepened the piscine odor of things. At length he asked, "Whose idea was it to leave the job to the police? Yours or your father's?"

The question discomfited Mock Quan. His eyes narrowed; he exhaled smoke in a thin jet. "I am not privileged to sit on the council of elders."

"No, but your father is. And I'll wager you have his confidence as well as his ear, and that your powers of persuasion are considerable."

"Such matters are of no concern to you."

"They're of great concern to me. I was nearly shot, too, in Ross Alley. And I'm not as convinced as the police that Little Pete is behind the death of James Scarlett or the disappearance of Bing Ah Kee's remains."

Mock Quan made an odd hissing sound with his lips, a Chinese expression of anger and contempt. There was less oil and more steel in his voice when he spoke again. "You would do well to bow to the superior intelligence of the police, Mr. Quincannon. Lest your blood stain a Chinatown alley after all."

"I don't like warnings, Mock Quan."

"A humble Chinese warn a distinguished Occidental detective? They were merely words of caution and prudence."

Quincannon's smile was nothing more than a lip-stretch. He said, "I have no intention of leaving a single drop of my blood in Chinatown."

"Then you would be wise not to venture here again after the cloak of night has fallen." His smile was as specious as Quincannon's. So was the invitation which followed: "Will you join me in a cup of excellent rose-petal tea before you leave?"

"Another time, perhaps."

"Perhaps. *Ho hang la*—I hope you have a safe walk."

"Health and long life to you, too."

As he made his way out of the building, Quincannon felt a definite lift in spirits. The briny aroma had grown so strong that now he had a very good idea of its source, its species, and its cause.

Your hat, Mock Quan, he thought with grim humor. In your blasted hat!

Sabina said, "Mrs. Scarlett has taken to her bed with grief and the comfort of a bottle of creme de menthe. It made questioning her difficult, to say the least."

"Were you able to find out anything?"

"Little enough. Her husband, as far as she is aware, had no incriminating documents in his possession, nor does she know where he might have put such a document for safekeeping. And she has no recollection of his ever mentioning

Fowler Alley in her presence."

"I was afraid that would be the case."

"Judging from your expression, your visit to Fowler Alley proved enlightening."

"Not Fowler Alley; that piece of the puzzle is still elusive. My call at the Hip Sing Company."

She raised an eyebrow. "You went there? I don't see a puncture wound anywhere. No bullets fired or hatchets or knives thrown your way?"

"Bah. I've bearded fiercer lions in their dens than Mock Quan."

"Who is Mock Quan?"

"The son of Mock Don Yuen, new leader of the tong. A sly gent with delusions of grandeur and a hunger for power as great as Little Pete's. Unless I miss my guess, he is the murderer of James Scarlett and the near murderer of your devoted partner."

Sabina's other eyebrow arched even higher. "What led you to that conclusion?"

"His hat," Quincannon said.

"His—Are you quite serious, John?"

"Never more so. The gunman outside Blind Annie's Cellar wore a black slouch hat with a red what-do-you-call-it on top—"

"A *mow-yung*," Sabina said.

He frowned. "How do you know that?"

"And why shouldn't a woman know something you don't? A *mow-yung* is a symbol of high caste in Chinese society."

"That much I do know," Quincannon growled. "Coolie food sellers don't wear 'em and neither do the *boo how doy*. That's what has been bothering me about the assassin from the first. He wasn't a highbinder but an upper-class Chinese masquerading as one."

"How do you know it was Mock Quan?"

"I don't know it for sure. A hunch, a strong one. Mock Quan is ambitious, foolhardy, corrupt, and ruthless. He covets Little Pete's empire in Chinatown. He as much as said so."

"Why would he risk killing Scarlett himself?"

"If my hunch is correct, he's working at cross-purposes to those of his father and the Hip Sing elders. It's his plan to let Lieutenant Price and the flying squad finish off his enemies and then to take over Little Pete's position as crime boss— with or without the blessings of his father and the tong. He has allies in the Hip Sing, certainly, but none he trusted enough to do the job on Scarlett. He's the sort to have no qualms about committing cold-blooded murder."

"For the dual purpose of stirring up the police and si- lencing Scarlett? Mock Quan is behind the body snatching, too, if you're right."

"I'd bet five gold eagles on it," Quincannon agreed. "And another five he's at least partly responsible for the letter of Scarlett's found on the Kwong Dock highbinder who was killed by the police this morning."

"That's fresh news," Sabina said. "Tell me."

He told her.

"I wonder how Mock Quan could have managed such flummery as that?"

"I can think of one way."

"Yes," she said slowly, "so can I. But proving it may be difficult. The case against Mock Quan, too."

"I know it. But there has to be a way to expose him before the kettle boils over. His plan is mad, but madder ones have succeeded and will again." He began to pace the office. "If we only knew the significance of Fowler Alley . . . Did you manage to have a look around the Scarlett lodgings?"

Sabina nodded. "Scarlett kept a desk there, but it contained nothing revealing. I did learn one small item of interest from Mrs. Scarlett before she fell asleep. It answers one question, while posing another."

"Yes?"

"She was followed when she came to see us yesterday. She intended to mention the fact but she was too upset about her husband."

"Followed? Not by a Chinese?"

"No, a Caucasian. A stranger to her."

"What did he look like?"

"She wasn't able to get a clear look at him. A man in a blue suit was all the description she could provide."

Quincannon muttered, "Blue shadow, eh?"

"Evidently. Another Caucasian on the Hip Sing payroll, one of Mock Quan's allies. And the explanation of how Mock Quan was able to follow you on your rounds of the opium resorts."

"Mmm." Quincannon continued to pace for a time. Then, abruptly, he stopped and said, "Perhaps not such a *small* item of interest after all, my dear."

"Have you thought of something?"

"Been bitten by another hunch is more like it." He reached for his coat and derby.

"Where are you off to?"

"Scarlett's law offices. My search last night was hasty and it's possible I overlooked something of importance. Or rather, spent my time looking for the wrong thing."

No one else had passed through the portal marked *J. H. Scarlett, Attorney-at-Law* since Quincannon's nocturnal visit. Or if anyone had, it'd been without any further disturbance of the premises.

With a close curb on his impatience, he set about once more sifting through the lawyer's papers. He examined each document carefully, some more than once. The hunch that had bitten him had plenty of teeth: One name kept re-appearing in similar context, and the more he saw it, the more furiously his nimble brain clicked and whirred. When he stood at last from the desk, his smile and the profane oath he uttered through it had a wolfish satisfaction.

He was certain, now, that he knew most of what there was to know. The only piece of the game he didn't have, in fact, was the one that had eluded him since last night: Fowler Alley.

A sharp, chill wind blew along the alley's close confines. Litter swirled; pigtailed men and work-stooped women hurried on their errands, not half so many as there had been earlier. Quincannon sensed an urgency in their movements, an almost palpable tension in the air. Word had spread of the flying squad's planned raids and the law-abiding were eager to be off the streets before dark.

Quincannon walked slowly, hands buried in the pockets of his Chesterfield, his shoulders hunched and his head swiveling left and right. The buildings in the first block, with their grimy windows and indecipherable calligraphy, told him no more than they had earlier. He entered the second block, frustration mounting in him again.

He was halfway along when he noticed a high-sided black wagon drawn up in front of some sort of business establishment. A small cluster of citizens stood watching something being loaded into the rear of the wagon. Quincannon moved closer. He was taller than most Chinese; he could see over the tops of the watchers' heads as he neared. One clear look at the object being loaded and he fetched up in a sudden standstill.

Casket.

Hearse.

Undertaking parlor!

He turned swiftly, ran back on that side of the alley until he came to an opening between the buildings. A tunnel-like walkway brought him into a deeply rutted dirt passage that paralleled Fowler Alley. He counted buildings to the rear of the one that housed the undertaker's. The door there was neither barred nor latched; he pushed it open with his left hand, drawing his Navy Colt with his right, and entered the gloomy corridor within.

The sickish odor of formaldehyde dilated his nostrils, set him to breathing through his mouth as he eased along the hall. From the front of the building the singsong of Chinese dialect came to him, but back here there was no sound.

The lantern-lit chamber into which he emerged was empty except for rows of coffins, most of them plain, a few of the lacquered teakwood favored by the high-born and the wealthy. A tapestried doorway opened to the right. Quincannon went there, pushed the covering aside.

Here was the embalming room, the source of the formaldehyde odor. He crossed it, past a metal table, an herb cabinet, another cabinet in which needles, razors, and other tools of the mortician's trade gleamed, to where a row of three slender storage vaults were set into the wall. The first vault he opened was empty. The second contained the body of a very old Mandarin whose skin was so wrinkled he might have been mummified. Quincannon opened the third.

The body in this vault was also an old man's, but one who had lived a much more pampered life. It was dressed in an intricately embroidered robe of gold silk; the cheeks had been powdered, the thin drooping moustaches trimmed; a prayerbook was still clutched between the gnarled hands.

"Bing Ah Kee," Quincannon said under his breath, "or I'm not the master detective I believe I am."

He closed the vault, retraced his steps to the doorway, pushed the tapestry aside. And came face-to-face with a youngish individual wearing a stained leather apron over his blouse and pantaloons. The man let out a startled bleat and an oath or epithet that threatened to escalate into a full-fledged cry of alarm. As he turned to flee, voice just starting to rise, Quincannon tapped him with the barrel of his Navy at the spot where queue met scalp. Flight and cry both ended instantly.

Quincannon stepped over the fallen Chinese, hurried across the coffin room and into the rear corridor. Fortunately for him, he had the presence of mind to ease the outside door open and his head out for a look around, instead of rushing through. It saved him from having some tender and perhaps vital portion of his anatomy punctured by a bullet.

As it was, the gunman lying in wait in a nearby doorway fired too hastily; the slug thwacked into the wall several inches from Quincannon's head, which he quickly jerked back inside. There were no more shots. He stood tensely, listening. Was that the slap of footfalls? He edged the door open again and poked his head out at a lower point than the first time.

Footfalls, indeed. The assassin was on the run. Quincannon straightened and stepped outside, but before he could trigger a shot the black-outfitted figure vanished into the walkway to Fowler Alley.

Mock Quan, of course, in his highbinder's guise. The fact that he'd made this attempt at homicide in broad daylight was an indication of just how desperate Quincannon's discovery had made him. So was the craven way he'd taken flight after his first shot missed its mark.

That was the difference between despots such as Little Pete and would-be despots such as Mock Quan, Quincannon mused. Both were rapacious and reckless, but the true tyrant was too arrogant to give himself up to panic. The would-be tyrant was far easier to bring down because his arrogance was no more than a thin membrane over a shell of cowardice.

When Quincannon arrived at the Hall of Justice he found Price, Gentry, and a dozen other men of the flying squad already preparing for the night's assault on Chinatown. The basement assembly room was strewn with coils of rope, firemen's axes, sledgehammers, artillery, and bulletproof vests similar to the coats of chain mail worn by the *boo how doy*.

He drew the lieutenant aside and did some fast talking, the gist of which was that he had information which would render the raids unnecessary. Fifteen minutes later he was once again seated in the chief's office, holding court before the same three officers as on his previous visit. As he spoke, he noted that the expressions worn by the trio were more or less the same, too: Crowley's stern and disapproving, Price's intently thoughtful, Gentry's hostile.

None of them commented until he finished and leaned back in his chair. Then each spoke in rapid succession.

Crowley: "That's quite a tale, Quincannon."

Gentry: "Hogwash, I say."

Price: "Fact or fiction, we'll find out soon enough. I want my own look inside that undertaking parlor."

"What good will that do?" Gentry argued. "Even if Mock Quan is behind all that's happened, old Bing's bones will be long gone by the time we get there."

"I think not, Sergeant," Quincannon said. "Mock Quan likely has nowhere to move the body on short notice. And he won't destroy it for the same reason he didn't before—fear of the wrath of the gods and all of Chinatown. Even if he were able to remove the body, there are bound to be ties between him and the mortician. Put pressure on that party and his terror of tong reprisal will bring out the truth. I'll warrant the whole house of cards can be collapsed around Mock Quan in a few hours, and that he knows it as well as I do. I wouldn't be surprised to hear that he has already left the city—on the run ever since his bullet missed my head."

"Nor would I, if you're right," Price said. "And I'm beginning to believe you are."

The chief leaned forward. "You really think Mock Quan is capable of plotting such a scheme, Will?"

"I wouldn't have until now. He's sneaky and ruthless, yes, but not half so clever as Little Pete. Still . . ."

"The plan wasn't his alone," Quincannon said. "He had help in its devising."

"Help? Help from whom?"

"A blue shadow."

"What the devil are you talking about?"

"James Scarlett said two things before he was killed. One was 'Fowler Alley'; the other was 'blue shadow.' And the truth is, he was as afraid of a blue shadow as he was of Mock Quan. His guilty knowledge wasn't only of the body snatching, but of the identity of Mock Quan's partner—the man who followed Scarlett's wife to my offices yesterday and who arranged for Mock Quan to follow me in Chinatown last night."

"*What* partner?" Chief Crowley demanded. "What does blue shadow mean?"

"It means a shadowy person in blue," Quincannon said. "Not a plain blue suit, as the partner wore yesterday, but a blue uniform—a policeman's uniform." He paused dramatically. "One of the policemen in this room is Mock Quan's accomplice."

All three officers came to their feet as one. Gentry aimed a quivering forefinger as if it were the barrel of his sidearm. "Preposterous nonsense! How dare you accuse one of us—"

"You, Sergeant. I'm accusing *you*."

The smoky air fairly crackled. Price and Crowley were both staring at Gentry; the sergeant's eyes threw sparks at Quincannon. The cords in the short man's neck bulged. His color was a shade less purple than an eggplant's.

"It's a dirty lie!" he shouted.

"Cold, hard fact."

Price said with contained fury, "Can you prove this allegation, Quincannon?"

"I can, to your satisfaction. After I left here last night, I went to James Scarlett's law offices. They had already been searched sometime earlier, likely soon after Mrs. Scarlett visited my offices. At first I believed the job was done by one of the highbinders, hunting any incriminating evidence Scarlett may have had in his possession. But that wasn't the case. The search hadn't the stamp of the tong man; it was much more professionally conducted, as a policeman goes about such a frisk. Gentry's work, gentlemen."

"For the same reason?"

"More probably to look for evidence of his conspiracy with Mock Quan. If there was any such evidence, Gentry made off with it. He also made off with a letter written on Scarlett's stationery and signed by the attorney—the same letter you found on the Kwong Dock highbinder who was killed last night. Killed by Gentry, wasn't he? And the letter found by Gentry afterward?"

"Yes, by God. Right on both counts."

"He tried to put a knife in me!" Gentry cried. "You saw him, Lieutenant—"

"I saw nothing of the kind. I took your word for it."

"A clever attempt to tighten the frame against Little Pete," Quincannon said. "As was Gentry's constant urging of you and Chief Crowley to crush Pete and the Kwong Dock."

"Lies! Don't listen to him—"

The other two officers ignored him. Price said, "Go on, Quincannon."

"When Gentry searched Scarlett's offices he carried off any direct evidence he may have found, as I said. But he failed to notice indirect evidence just as damning. Scarlett's legal records indicate the sergeant was in the pay of the Hip Sing, just as Scarlett himself was, long *before* Gentry and Mock Quan cooked up their takeover scheme. He was mixed up in nearly all of the cases in which Scarlett successfully defended a Hip Sing member. In some, his testimony—false or distorted—resulted in acquittal. In others, it's plain that he suppressed evidence or suborned perjury or both."

Gentry started toward Quincannon with murder in his eye. "If there are any such lies in Scarlett's records, *you* put them there, you damned flycop! You're the one trying to pull a frame—"

Price stepped in front of him. "Stand where you are, Sergeant," he said in a voice that brooked no disobedience.

Quincannon went on, "Another piece of proof: Last night, if you recall, Gentry suggested taking the flying squad to find evidence of Little Pete's guilt in Scarlett's death—the bogus evidence he later planted himself. He also said, 'Evidence to point to the cold storage where old Bing's bones are stashed.' Yet for all any of us knew at that point, the body might have been burned, or buried, or weighted and cast into the Bay, or had any of a dozen other things done with it or to it. Why would he use the specific term 'cold storage' unless he knew that was what had been done with old Bing's remains?"

Gentry called him a name and tried once again to mount a

charge. The lieutenant shoved him back, none too gently.

"And if all that isn't sufficient validation of his duplicity," Quincannon concluded, "there is Mrs. Scarlett. She had a good look at the man who followed her yesterday and can easily identify him." A bald lie, this, but an effective capper nonetheless. "Gentry had no official reason to be following the woman, did he, Lieutenant?"

"No," Price said darkly, "he didn't."

The chief stalked around his desk and fixed Gentry with a gimlet eye. "A damned highbinder no better than Little Pete or Mock Quan—is that what you are, Gentry?"

"No! No, I swear—"

"Because if so I'll see your mangy hide strung from the highest flagpole in the city."

Gentry shook his head, his eyes rolling, sweat shining on his forehead and cheeks. He was still wagging his head as Quincannon judiciously slipped out and went to find a quiet corner where he could smoke his pipe and enjoy his vindication.

"Gentry's shell was no harder to crack than a Dungeness crab's," he told Sabina a while later. "It took Crowley and Price less than fifteen minutes to break him wide open."

"No doubt with the aid of some gentle persuasion."

"Have you ever known the blue shadows to use another kind?"

She laughed. "What was his motive? Power and greed, the same as Mock Quan's?"

"Those, and severe gambling losses. Which was why he sold himself to the Hip Sing in the first place. It seems the sergeant has a fondness for roulette and fan-tan, and little skill at any game of chance."

"Well, I must say you've plenty of skill at your particular game."

"I have, haven't I?"

"Exceeded only by your modesty," Sabina said. "Still, it's thanks to you that the crisis in Chinatown has been averted."

"For the time being. Until another, smarter Mock Quan emerges or something or someone else lights the fuse. Mark my words—one of these days, the whole Quarter will go up in flames."

"You may be right. In any event, this is one case it will be a relief, if not a pleasure, to mark closed. We'll waive Mrs. Scarlett's fee, of course. I'll post a letter to her tomorrow—Why are you looking at me that way?"

Quincannon was aghast. He said, "Waive her fee?"

"It's the least we can do for the poor woman."

"Sabina, have you forgotten that I was shot at twice and almost killed? As well as made to trek through low Chinatown alleys, prowl opium dens, and invade an undertaking parlor in search of a snatched corpse?"

"I haven't forgotten."

"Well, then? All of that, not to mention a near tarnish on our fine reputation as detectives, for not so much as a copper cent?"

"I'm afraid so, my erstwhile Scot. It's the proper thing to do and you know it."

"Bah. I know nothing of the kind."

Her expression softened. After a silence during which she seemed to be doing a bit of weighing and balancing, she said, "I suppose you should have one small reward, at least."

"Yes? And what would that be?"

"An evening out with me, if you like. Dinner at the Palace, then a performance of Gilbert and Sullivan's new opera at the Tivoli Theater. I've been wanting to see *Patience* since it opened."

Quincannon's momentary gloom evaporated as swiftly as

an ice cube in a furnace. Smiling jauntily, he said, "And after the performance?"

"You may escort me to my flat."

"And after that?"

Sabina sighed. "You never give up, do you, John Quincannon?"

"Never. For my intentions are honorable, my passions sweet and pure. No, never, as long as a breath remains in my body."

The word Sabina uttered in response to that was heartfelt and decidedly unladylike.

Wishful Thinking

When I got home from work, a little after six as usual, Jerry
Macklin was sitting slumped on his front porch. Head down,
long arms hanging loose between his knees. Uh-oh, I thought.
I put the car in the garage and walked back down the driveway
and across the lawn strip onto the Macklins' property.

"Hi there, Jerry."

He looked up. "Oh, hello, Frank."

"Hot enough for you?"

"Hot," he said. "Yes, it's hot."

"Only June and already in the nineties every day. Looks
like we're in for another blistering summer."

"I guess we are."

"How about coming over for a beer before supper?"

He waggled his head. He's long and loose, Jerry, with
about twice as much neck as anybody else. When he shakes
his big head, it's like watching a bulbous flower bob at the end
of a stalk. As always these days, his expression was morose.
He used to smile a lot, but not much since his accident.
About a year ago he fell off a roof while on his job as a
building inspector, damaged some nerves and vertebrae in
his back, and was now on permanent disability.

"I killed Verna a little while ago," he said.

"Is that right?"

"She's in the kitchen. Dead on the kitchen floor."

"Uh-huh," I said.

"We had another big fight and I went and got my old service pistol out of the attic. She didn't even notice when I

42

came back down with it, just started in ragging on me again. I shot her right after she called me a useless bum for about the thousandth time."

"Well," I said. Then I said, "A gun's a good way to do it, I guess."

"The best way," Jerry said. "All the other ways, they're too uncertain or too bloody. A pistol really is the best."

"Well, I ought to be getting on home."

"I wonder if I should call the police."

"I wouldn't do that if I were you, Jerry."

"No?"

"Wouldn't be a good idea."

"Hot day like this, maybe I—"

"Jerry!" Verna's voice, from inside the house. Loud and demanding, but with a whiny note underneath. "How many times do I have to ask you to come in here and help me with supper? The potatoes need peeling."

"Damn," Jerry said.

Sweat had begun to run on me; I mopped my face with my handkerchief. "If you feel like it," I said, "we can have that beer later on."

"Sure, okay."

"I'll be in the yard after supper. Come over anytime."

His head wobbled again, up and down this time. Then he stood, wincing on account of his back, and shuffled into his house, and I walked back across and into mine. Mary Ellen was in the kitchen, cutting up something small and green by the sink. Cilantro, from the smell of it.

"I saw you through the window," she said. "What were you talking to Jerry about?"

"Three guesses."

"Oh, Lord. I suppose he killed Verna again."

"Yep."

"Where and how this time?"

"In the kitchen. With his service pistol."

"That man. Three times now, or is it four?"

"Four."

"Other people have nice normal neighbors. We have to have a crazy person living next door."

"Jerry's harmless, you know that. He was as normal as anybody before he fell off that roof."

"Harmless," Mary Ellen said. "Famous last words."

I went over and kissed her neck. Damp, but it still tasted pretty good. "What're you making there?"

"Ceviche."

"What's ceviche?"

"Cold fish soup. Mexican style."

"Sounds awful."

"It isn't. You've had it before."

"Did I like it?"

"You loved it."

"Sounds wonderful, then. I'm going to have a beer. You want one?"

"I don't think so." Pretty soon she said, "He really ought to see somebody."

"Who?"

"Jerry."

"See who? You mean a head doctor?"

"Yes. Before he really does do something to Verna."

"Come on, honey. Jerry can't even bring himself to step on a bug. And Verna's enough to drive any man a little crazy. Either she's mired in one of her funks or on a rampage about something or other. And she's always telling him how worthless and lazy she thinks he is."

"She has a point," Mary Ellen said. "All he does all day is sit around drinking beer and staring at the tube."

"Well, with his back the way it is—"

"His back doesn't seem to bother him when he decides to work in his garden."

"Hey, I thought you liked Jerry."

"I do like Jerry. It's just that I can see Verna's side, the woman's side. He was no ball of fire before the accident, and he's never let her have children—"

"That's her story. He says he's sterile."

"Well, whatever. I still say she has some justification for being moody and short-tempered, especially in this heat."

"I suppose."

"Anyhow," Mary Ellen said, "her moods don't give Jerry the right to keep pretending he's killed her. And I don't care how harmless he seems to be, he could snap someday. People who have violent fantasies often do. Every day you read about something like that in the papers or see it on the TV news."

"'Violent fantasies' is too strong a term in Jerry's case."

"What else would you call them?"

"He doesn't sit around all day thinking about killing Verna. I got that much out of him after he scared hell out of me the first time. They have a fight and he goes out on the porch and sulks and that's when he imagines her dead. And only once in a while. It's more like . . . wishful thinking."

"Even so, it's not healthy and it's potentially dangerous. I wonder if Verna knows."

"Probably not, or she'd be making his life even more miserable. We can hear most of what she yells at him all the way over here as it is."

"Somebody ought to tell her."

"You're not thinking of doing it? You don't even like the woman." Which was true. Jerry and I were friendly enough, to the point of going fishing together a few times, but the four of us had never done couples things. Verna wasn't interested.

Didn't seem to want much to do with Mary Ellen or me. Or anyone else, for that matter, except a couple of old woman friends.

"I might go over and talk to her," Mary Ellen said. "Express concern about Jerry's behavior, if nothing more."

"I think it'd be a mistake."

"Do you? Well, you're probably right."

"So you're going to do it anyway."

"Not necessarily. I'll have to think about it."

Mary Ellen went over to talk to Verna two days later. It was a Saturday and Jerry'd gone off somewhere in their car. I was on the front porch fixing a loose shutter when she left, and still there and still fixing when she came back less than ten minutes later.

"That was fast," I said.

"She didn't want to talk to me." Mary Ellen looked and sounded miffed. "She was barely even civil."

"Did you tell her about Jerry's wishful thinking?"

"No. I didn't have a chance."

"What did you say to her?"

"Hardly anything except that we were concerned about Jerry."

"We," I said. "As in me too."

"Yes, we. She shut me off right there. As much as told me to mind my own business."

"Well?" I said gently.

"Oh, all right, maybe we should. It's her life, after all. And it'll be as much her fault as Jerry's if he suddenly decides to make his wish come true."

Jerry killed Verna three more times in July. Kitchen again, their bedroom, the backyard. Tenderizing mallet, clock radio, manual strangulation—so I guess he'd decided a gun wasn't the best way after all. He seemed to grow more and more morose as the summer wore on, while Verna grew more and more sullen and contentious. The heat wave we were suffering through didn't help matters any. The temperatures were up around one hundred degrees half the days that month and everybody was bothered in one way or another.

Jerry came over one evening in early August while Mary Ellen and I were having fruit salad under the big elm in our yard. He had a six-pack under one arm and a look on his face that was half hunted, half depressed.

"Verna's on another rampage," he said. "I had to get out of there. Okay if I sit with you folks for a while?"

"Pull up a chair," I said. At least he wasn't going to tell us he'd killed her again.

Mary Ellen asked him if he'd like some fruit salad, and he said no, he guessed fruit and yogurt wouldn't mix with beer. He opened a can and drank half of it at a gulp. It wasn't his first of the day by any means.

"I don't know how much more of that woman I can take," he said.

"That bad, huh?"

"That bad. Morning, noon, and night—she never gives me a minute's peace any more."

Mary Ellen said, "Well, there's a simple solution, Jerry."

"Divorce? She won't give me one. Says she'll fight it if I file, take me for everything she can if it goes through."

"Some women hate the idea of living alone."

Jerry's head waggled on its neck-stalk. "It isn't that," he said. "Verna doesn't believe in divorce. Never has, never will. Till death do us part—that's what she believes in."

"So what're you going to do?" I asked him.

"Man, I just don't know. I'm at my wits' end." He drank

47

the rest of his beer in broody silence. Then he unfolded, wincing, to his feet. "Think I'll go back home now. Have a look in the attic."

"The attic?"

"See if I can find my old service pistol. A gun really is the best way to do it, you know."

After he was gone Mary Ellen said, "I don't like this, Frank. He's getting crazier all the time."

"Oh, come on."

"He'll go through with it one of these days. You mark my words."

"If that's the way you feel," I said, "why don't you try talking to Verna again? Warn her."

"I would if I thought she'd listen. But I know she won't."

"What else is there to do, then?"

"You could try talking to Jerry. Try to convince him to see a doctor."

"It wouldn't do any good. He doesn't think he needs help, any more than Verna does."

"At least try. Please, Frank."

"All right, I'll try. Tomorrow night, after work."

When I came home the next sweltering evening, one of the Macklins was sitting slumped on the front porch. But it wasn't Jerry, it was Verna. Head down, hands hanging between her knees. It surprised me so much I nearly swerved the car off onto our lawn. Verna almost never sat out on their front porch, alone or otherwise. She preferred the glassed-in back porch because it was air-conditioned.

The day had been another hundred-plus scorcher, and I was tired and soggy and I wanted a shower and a beer in the worst way. But I'd promised Mary Ellen I'd talk to Jerry—and it puzzled me about Verna sitting on the porch that way.

So I went straight over there from the garage.

Verna looked up when I said hello. Her round, plain face was red with prickly heat and her colorless hair hung limp and sweat-plastered to her skin. There was a funny look in her eyes and around her mouth, a look that made me feel uneasy.

"Frank," she said. "Lord, it's hot, isn't it?"

"And no relief in sight. Where's Jerry?"

"In the house."

"Busy? I'd like to talk to him."

"You can't."

"No? How come?"

"He's dead."

"What?"

"Dead," she said. "I killed him."

I wasn't hot anymore; it was as if I'd been doused with ice water. "Killed him? Jesus, Verna—"

"We had a fight and I went and got his service pistol and shot him in the back of the head while he was watching TV."

"When?" It was all I could think of to say.

"Little while ago."

"The police . . . have you called the police?"

"No."

"Then I'd better—"

The screen door popped open with a sudden creaking sound. I jerked my gaze that way, and Jerry was standing there big as life. "Hey, Frank," he said.

I gaped at him with my mouth hanging open.

"Look like you could use a cold one. You too, Verna."

Neither of us said anything.

Jerry said, "I'll get one for each of us," and the screen door banged shut.

I looked at Verna again. She was still sitting in the same

posture, head down, staring at the steps with that funny look on her face.

"I know about him killing me all the time," she said. "Did you think I didn't know, didn't hear him saying it?"

There were no words in my head. I closed my mouth.

"I wanted to see how it felt to kill him the same way," Verna said. "And you know what? It felt good."

I backed down the steps, started to turn away. But I was still looking at her and I saw her head come up, I saw the odd little smile that changed the shape of her mouth.

"Good," she said, "but not good enough."

I went home. Mary Ellen was upstairs, taking a shower. When she came out I told her what had just happened.

"My God, Frank. The heat's made her as crazy as he is. They're two of a kind."

"No," I said, "they're not. They're not the same at all."

"What do you mean?"

I didn't tell her what I meant. I didn't have to, because just then in the hot, dead stillness we both heard the crack of the pistol shot from next door.

Shade Work

Johnny Shade blew into San Francisco on the first day of summer. He went there every year, when he had the finances; it was a good place to find action on account of the heavy convention business. Usually he went a little later in the summer, around mid-July, when there were fifteen or twenty thousand conventioneers wandering around, a high percentage of them with money in their pockets and a willingness to lay some of it down on a poker table. You could take your time then, weed out the deadheads and the short-money scratchers. Pick your vic.

But this year was different. This year he couldn't afford to wait around or take his time. He had three thousand in his kick that he'd scored in Denver, and he needed to parlay that into ten grand—fast. Ten grand would buy him into a big con Elk Tracy and some other boys were setting up in Louisville. A classic big-store con, even more elaborate than the one Newman and Redford had pulled off in *The Sting*, Johnny's favorite flick. Elk needed a string of twenty and a nut of two hundred thousand to set it up right; that was the reason for the ten-grand buy-in. The guaranteed net was two million. Ten grand buys you a hundred, minimum. Johnny Shade had been a card mechanic and cheat for nearly two decades and he'd never held that much cash in his hands at one time. Not even close to that much.

He was a small-time grifter and he knew it. A single-o, traveling around the country on his own because he preferred it that way, looking for action wherever he could find it. But it was never heavy action, never the big score. Stud and draw games in hotel rooms with marks who never seemed to want to lose more than a few hundred at a sitting. He wasn't a good enough mechanic to play in even a medium-stakes game and hope to get away with crimps or hops or overhand run-ups or Greek-deals or hand-mucks or any of the other shuffling or dealing cheats. He just didn't have the fingers for it. So mostly he relied on his specialty, shade work, which was how he'd come to be called Johnny Shade. He even signed hotel registers as Johnny Shade nowadays, instead of the name he'd been born with. A kind of private joke.

Shade work was fine in small games. Most amateurs never thought to examine or riffle-test a deck when he ran a fresh one in, because it was always in its cellophane wrapper with the manufacturer's seal unbroken. The few who did check the cards didn't spot the gaff on account of they were looking for blisters, shaved edges, blockout or cutout work—the most common methods of marking a deck. They didn't know about the more sophisticated methods like flash or shade work. In Johnny's case, they probably wouldn't have spotted the shade gaff if they had known, not the way he did it.

He had it down to a science. He diluted blue and red aniline dye with alcohol until he had the lightest possible tint, then used a camel's hair brush to wash over a small section of the back pattern of each card in a Bee or Bicycle deck. The dye wouldn't show on the red or blue portion of the card back, but it tinted the white part just lightly enough so you could see it if you knew what to look for. And he had eyesight almost as good as Clark Kent's. He could spot his shade work on a vic's cards across the table in poor light without even squinting.

But the high-rollers knew about shade work, just as they knew about every other scam a professional hustler could come up with. You couldn't fool them, so you couldn't steal their money. If you were Johnny Shade, you had to content yourself with low-rollers and deadheads, with pocket and traveling cash instead of the big score.

He was tired of the game, that was the thing. He'd been at it too long, lived on the far edge of riches too long, been a single-o grifter too long. He wanted a slice of the good life. Ten grand buys a hundred. With a hundred thousand he could travel first-class, wine and dine and bed first-class women, take his time finding new action—maybe even set up a big con of his own. Or find a partner and work some of the fancier short cons. Lots of options, as long as a guy had real money in his kick.

First, though, he had to parlay his Denver three K into ten K. Then he could hop a plane for Louisville and look up Elk Tracy. Ten days . . . that was all the time he had before Elk closed out his string. Ten days to pick the right vics, set up two or three or however many games it took him to net the seven thousand.

He found his first set of marks his first night in Frisco. That was a good omen. His luck was going to change; he could feel it.

Most weeks in the summer there was a convention going on at the Hotel Nob Hill, off Union Square. He walked in there on this night, and the first thing he saw was a banner that said WELCOME FIDDLERS in great big letters. Hick musicians, or maybe some kind of organization for people who were into cornball music. Just his type of crowd. Just his type of mark.

He hung out in the bar, nursing a beer, circulating, keeping his ears open. There were certain words he listened for and "poker" was one of them. One of four guys in a booth used it, and when he sidled closer he saw that they were all wearing badges with FIDDLER on them and their names and the cities they were from written underneath. They were talking the right talk: stud poker, bragging about how good they were at it, getting ready for a game. Ripe meat. All he had to do was finagle his way among them, get himself invited to join the play if the set-up and the stakes were right.

He was good at finagling. He had the gift of gab, and a face like a Baptist preacher's, and a winning smile. First he sat himself down at a table near their booth. Then he contrived to jostle a waitress and spill a fresh round of beers she was bringing to them. He offered to pay for the drinks, flashed his wallet so they could see that he was flush. Chatted them up a little, taking it slow, feeling his way.

One of the fiddlers bought him a beer, then he bought them all another round. That got him the invitation to join them. Right away he laid on the oil about being in town for a convention himself, the old birds of a feather routine. They shook hands all around. Dave from Cleveland, Mitch from Los Angeles, Verne from Cedar Rapids, Harry from Bayonne. And Johnny from Denver. He didn't even have to maneuver the talk back to cards. They weren't interested in his convention or their own, or San Francisco, or any other kind of small talk; they were interested in poker. He played some himself, he said. Nothing he liked better than five-stud or draw. No wild-card games, none of that crap; he was a purist. So were they.

"We're thinking about getting up a game," Harry from Bayonne said. "You feel like sitting in, Johnny?"

"I guess I wouldn't mind," he said. "Depending on the stakes. Nothing too rich for my blood." He showed them his best smile. "Then again, nothing too small, either. Poker's no good unless you make it interesting, right?"

If they'd insisted on penny-ante or buck-limit, he'd have

backed out and gone looking elsewhere. But they were sports: table stakes, ten-buck limit per bet, no limit on raises. They looked like they could afford that kind of action. Fiddle-music jerks, maybe, but well-dressed and reasonably well-heeled. He caught a glimpse of a full wallet when Mitch from L.A. bought another round. Might be as much as four or five grand among the four of them.

Verne from Cedar Rapids said he had a deck of cards in his room; they could play there. Johnny said, "Sounds good. How about if we go buy a couple more decks in the gift shop. Nothing like the feel of a new deck after a while."

They all thought that was a good idea. Everybody drank up and they went together to the gift shop. All Johnny had to do was make sure the cards they bought were Bicycle, one of the two most common brands; he had four shaded Bicycle decks in his pocket, two blue-backs and two red-backs. Then they all rode upstairs to Verne from Cedar Rapids's room and shed their coats and jackets and got down to business.

Johnny played it straight for a while, card-counting, making conservative bets, getting a feel for the way the four marks played. Only one of them was reckless: Mitch from L.A., the one with the fattest wallet. He'd have liked two or three of that type, but one was better than none. One was all he needed.

After an hour and a half he was ahead about a hundred and Mitch from L.A. was the big winner, betting hard, bluffing at least part of the time. Better and better. Time to bring in one of his shaded decks. That was easy, too. They'd let him hold the decks they'd bought downstairs; simple for him to bring out one of his own instead.

He didn't open it himself. You always let one of the marks do that, so the mark could look it over and see that it was still sealed in cellophane with the manufacturer's stamp on top intact. The stamp was the main thing to the mark, the one thing you never touched when you were fixing a deck. What they didn't figure on was what you'd done: You carefully opened the cellophane wrapper along the bottom and slid out the card box. Then you opened the box along one side, prying the glued flaps apart with a razor blade. Once you'd shaded the cards, you resealed the box with rubber cement, slipped it back into the cellophane sleeve, refolded the sleeve ends along the original creases, and resealed them with a drop of glue. When you did the job right—and Johnny Shade was a master—nobody could tell that the package had been tampered with. Sure as hell not a fiddler named Dave from Cleveland, the one who opened the gimmicked deck.

The light was pretty good in there; Johnny could read his shade work with no more than a casual glance at the hands as they were dealt out. He took a couple of medium-sized pots, worked his winnings up to around five hundred, biding his time until both he and Mitch from L.A. drew big hands on the same deal. It finally happened about 10:30, on a hand of jacks-or-better. Harry from Bayonne was dealing; Johnny was on his left. Mitch from L.A. drew a pat full house, aces over fives. Johnny scored trip deuces. When he glanced over at the rest of the deck, he saw that the top card—his card on the draw—was the fourth deuce. Beautiful. A set-up like this was always better when you weren't the dealer, didn't have to deal seconds or anything like that to win the pot. Just read the shade and it was yours.

Mitch from L.A. bet ten and Johnny raised him and Mitch raised back. Verne from Cedar Rapids stayed while the other two dropped, which made Johnny smile inside. Verne owned four high spades in sequence and was gambling on a one-card draw to fill a royal or a straight flush. But there was no way he was going to get it because Mitch had his spade ace and

Johnny had his spade nine. The best he could do was a loser flush. Johnny raised again, and Mitch raised back, and Verne hung in stubborn. There was nearly a grand in the pot when Mitch finally called.

Johnny took just the one card on the draw, to make the others think he was betting two pair. Mitch would think that even if Johnny caught a full house, his would be higher because he had aces up; so Mitch would bet hot and heavy. Which he did. Verne from Cedar Rapids had caught his spade flush and hung in there for a while, driving the pot even higher, until he finally realized his flush wasn't going to beat what Johnny and Mitch were betting; then he dropped. Mitch kept right on working his full boat, raising each time Johnny raised, until he was forced to call when his cash pile ran down to a lone tenspot. That last ten lifted the total in the pot to twenty-two hundred bucks.

Johnny grinned and said, "Read 'em and weep, gentlemen," and fanned out his four deuces face up. Mitch from L.A. didn't say a word; he just dropped his cards and looked around at the others. None of them had anything to say, either. Johnny grinned again and said, "My lucky night," and reached for the pot.

Reaching for it was as far as he got.

Harry from Bayonne closed a big paw over his right wrist; Dave from Cleveland did the same with his left wrist. They held him like that, his hands imprisoned flat on the table.

"What the hell's the idea?" Johnny said.

Nobody answered him. Mitch from L.A. swept the cards together and then began to examine them one at a time, holding each card up close to his eyes.

Harry from Bayonne said, "What is it, shade work?"

"Right. Real professional job."

"Thought so. I'm pretty good at spotting blockout and

cutout work. And I didn't feel any blisters or edge or sand work."

"At first I figured he might be one of the white-on-white boys," Verne from Cedar Rapids said. "You know, used whiteout fluid on the white borders. Then I tumbled to the shading."

"Nice resealing on that card box, Johnny," Dave from Cleveland said. "If I hadn't known it was a gimmicked deck, I wouldn't have spotted it."

Johnny gawped. "You knew?" he said. "You all *knew?*"

"Oh sure," Mitch from L.A. said. "As soon as you moved in on us down in the bar."

"But—but—why did you . . . ?"

"We wanted to see what kind of hustler you were, how you worked your scam. You might call it professional curiosity."

"Christ. Who are you guys?"

They told him. And Johnny Shade groaned and put his head in his hands. He knew then that his luck had changed, all right—all for the bad. That he was never going to make the big score, in Louisville or anywhere else. That he might not even be much good as a small-time grifter any more. Once word of this got out, he'd be a laughingstock from coast to coast. And word *would* get out. These four would see to that.

They didn't belong to some hick music group. They weren't fiddlers; they were FIDDLERS, part of a newly formed nationwide professional organization. Fraud Identification Detectives, Domestic Law Enforcement Ranks.

Vice cops. He'd tried to run a gambling scam at a convention of vice cops . . .

I Think I Will Not Hang Myself Today

The leaves on the trees were dying.

She had noted that before, of course; neither her mind nor her powers of observation had been eroded by the passing years. But this morning, seen from her bedroom window, it seemed somehow a sudden thing, as if the maples and Japanese elms had changed color overnight, from bright green to red and brittle gold. Just yesterday it had been summer, now all at once it was autumn.

John had been taken from her on an October afternoon. It would be fitting if autumn were her time, too.

Perhaps today, she thought. Why not today?

For a while longer, Miranda stood looking out at the cold morning, the sky more gray than blue. Wind rattled the frail leaves, now and then tore one loose and swirled it to the ground. Even from a distance, the maple leaves resembled withered hands, their veins and skeletal bone structure clearly visible. The wind, blowing from east to west, sent the fallen ones skittering across the lawn and its bordering flower beds, piled them in heaps along the wall of the old barn.

Looking at the barn this morning filled her with sadness. Once, when John was alive, the skirling whine of his power saws and the fine, fresh smells of sawdust and wood stain and lemon oil made the barn seem alive, as sturdy and indestructible as the beautiful furniture that came from his workshop. Now it was a sagging shell, a lonely place of drafts and shadows and ghosts, its high center beam like the crosspiece of a gallows.

So little left, she thought as she turned from the window. John gone these many years. Moira gone—no family left at all. Lord Byron gone six months, and as much as she missed the little Sealyham's companionship, she hadn't the heart to replace him with another pet. Gone, too, were most of her friends. And the pleasures of teaching grammar and classic English literature, the satisfaction that came from helping to shape young minds. ("We're sorry, Mrs. Halliday, but you know the mandatory retirement age in our district is sixty-five.") For a time there had been a few students to privately tutor, but none had come since last spring. County library cutbacks had ended her volunteer work at the local branch. The arthritis made it all but impossible for her to continue her sewing projects for homeless children. Even Mrs. Boyer in the next block had found someone younger and stronger to babysit her two preschoolers.

The loneliness had been endurable when she was needed, really needed. Being able to help others had given some meaning and purpose to her life. Now, though, she had become the needy one, requiring help with the cleaning, the yardwork, her weekly grocery shopping. All too soon, she would no longer be able to drive her car, and then she would be housebound, totally dependent on others. If that happened . . .

No, she thought, it mustn't. I'm sorry, John, but it mustn't.

She thought again of the old barn, his workshop, the long, high rafter beam. When it had become clear and irrefutable what she must one day do, there had never been any question as to the method. Mr. Gilbert Chesterton had seen to that. She had bought the rope that very day, and it was still out there waiting. She would have to stand on a ladder in order to loop it around the beam—not an easy task, even though the knot had long ago been tied. But she would manage. She had always managed, hadn't she? Supremely capable, John had called her. That, and the most determined woman he had ever known; once her mind was made up, nothing would change it. Yes, and the end would be quick and she would not suffer. No one should ever have to suffer when the time came.

Chesterton's lines ran through her mind again:

> The strangest whim has seized me
> . . . . After all
> I think I will not hang myself today.

She had first come across "A Ballade of Suicide," one of his minor works, when she was a girl, and there had been something so haunting in those three lines that she had never forgotten them. One day, she would alter the last of the lines by deleting the word "not." This day, perhaps . . .

Miranda bathed and dressed and brushed her hair, which she kept short and wavy in the fashion John had liked. Satisfied with her appearance, she made her way downstairs and fixed a somewhat larger breakfast than usual—a soft-boiled egg to go with her habitual tea and toast. Then she washed the dishes—her hands were not paining too badly this morning—and entered the living room.

John had built every stick of furniture in there, of cherry wood and walnut. Tables, chairs, sofa and loveseat, sideboard, the tall cabinet that contained his collection of rifles and handguns. (She hated guns, but she had been unable to bring herself to rid the house of anything that had belonged to him.) Handcrafted furniture had been both his vocation and his hobby. An artist with wood, John Halliday. Everyone said so. She had loved to watch him work, to help him in his shop and to learn from him some of the finer points of his craft.

The photograph of John in his Navy uniform was centered on the fireplace mantel. She picked it up, looked at it until his lean, dark face began to blur, then replaced it. She dried her eyes and peered at the other framed photos that flanked his.

Mother, so slender and fragile, the black velvet-banded cameo she'd always worn hiding the grease burn on her throat. Father in cap and gown at one of his college graduation ceremonies, looking as young as one of his students. Moira and herself at ages four and seven, all dressed up for some occasion or other, and wasn't it odd how much prettier she had been as a child, when it was Moira who had grown into such a beautiful woman? Uncle Leon, his mouth full of the foul pipe he favored, and Aunt Gwen as round and white as the Pillsbury Doughboy. Gone, all gone. Dust. Sweet-sad memories and scattered specks of dust.

Miranda moved to the bookcases on the near side of the fireplace. Her domain; John had never been much of a reader, despite her best efforts. Plato, Thomas Aquinas, Shakespeare, Chaucer. Scott, Dickens, Hawthorne, the Brontë sisters, Stevenson. Browning and Byron and Eliot and Edna St. Vincent Millay. Nearly a dozen volumes of fiction and nonfiction by Chesterton, always her favorite. Oscar Wilde, so amusing and ironic—

The phone was ringing.

She may have heard the first ring, or the bell may have sounded two or three times before she grew aware of it; she wasn't quite sure. She went to answer it.

"Miranda, dear, how are you?"

"Oh, hello, Patrice."

"You sound a bit melancholy this morning. Is everything all right?"

"Yes. You mustn't worry about me."

"But I do. You know I do."

Miranda knew it all too well. Patrice was one of her oldest friends, but their closeness was neither deep nor confiding. Patrice's life had been one long, smooth sail, empty of tragedy of any kind; she had never needed anyone outside her immediate family. And ever since Miranda's own tragic loss, Patrice's friendship and concern had been tinged with thinly concealed pity.

"I called to invite you to lunch tomorrow," Patrice said. "You need to get out more, and lunch at the Shady Grove Inn is just the ticket. My treat."

"That's good of you, but I don't believe I'll be able to accept."

"Other plans, dear?"

"I . . . may not be here tomorrow."

"Oh? Going away somewhere?"

"Possibly. It's not quite certain yet."

"May I ask where and with whom?"

"I'd rather not say."

"Of course, I understand. But talking about something in advance really doesn't prevent it from happening, you know."

"It can," Miranda said. "Sometimes it can."

"Well, you must tell me all about it afterward."

"It won't be a secret, Patrice. I can promise you that."

They talked a few minutes longer. Or rather, Patrice talked, mostly about her grandchildren. Miranda only half listened. It seemed quite cold in the house now, despite the fact that she had turned up the heat when she came downstairs. Imagination? No, she could hear the wind in the eaves, gusting more strongly than before, and when that happened the house always felt drafty.

When Patrice finally said goodbye, Miranda returned to the living room and put on the gas-log flame in the fireplace. She sat in front of it with a copy of Wilde's *The Importance of Being Earnest* open on her lap and tried to read. She couldn't seem to concentrate. I wish I had something else to do, she thought, something useful or important.

Well, she thought then, there is something, isn't there? Out in the barn?

But she was not ready to go out there yet. Not just yet. She picked up Wilde and tried again to focus on his words.

She was dozing when the doorbell rang. Dreaming about something pleasant, something to do with John and their honeymoon in the Caribbean, but the jarring sound of the bell drove it away. A visitor? She so seldom had visitors these days. The prospect hurried her steps to the door.

But it wasn't a visitor; it was Dwayne, the mailman, on the porch outside. "Morning, Miz Halliday," he said. "More mail than usual today so I thought I'd bring it up, save you the trouble."

"That was good of you, Dwayne."

"Catalogues, mostly. Not even the end of October and already we got piles of Christmas catalogues. Seems like they start sending 'em out earlier every year."

"Yes, it does."

He handed over the thick stack, being cautious about it because he knew of her arthritis. "You going out today, Miz Halliday?"

"I may, yes. Why do you ask?"

"Well, it's pretty cold out. Wind's got ice in it, first breath of winter. Real pneumonia weather. Better bundle up warm if you do go out."

"I will, thank you."

He wished her a good morning and left her alone again.

Miranda sifted through her mail. No personal letters, of course. Just two bills and three solicitations, one of the solicitations addressed to "Maranda Holiday." She laid the bills, unopened, on the kitchen table, put the solicitations in the trash and the catalogues in the recycle box.

Except for the wind, the house was very quiet.

And still unwarm.

And so empty.

In her sewing room, she removed the letter—three pages, carefully folded—from the bottom drawer of her desk. She had written it quite a long time ago, but she could have quoted it verbatim. The wind gusted noisily as she started out with it, rattling shingles and shutters, and she remembered what Dwayne had said about bundling up warm. The front hall closet yielded her heaviest wool coat and a pair of fleece-lined gloves. She had the coat over her shoulders, the letter tucked into one of the pockets, when the phone rang again.

"Mrs. Halliday? This is Sally Boyer?"

"Yes, Mrs. Boyer."

"I wonder if I could ask a big favor? I know it's short notice and I haven't been in touch in a while, but if you could help us out I'd really appreciate it?" Mrs. Boyer was one of those individuals who turn statements into questions by a rising interrogative inflection on the last few words of a sentence. More than once Miranda had been tempted to help her correct this irritating habit, but it would have been impolite to bring it up herself.

"What is the favor?"

"Could you babysit for us tonight? My husband has a business dinner, a client and his wife from Los Angeles who showed up without any advance warning? Well, he thinks it's important for me to join them and our regular sitter has band practice tonight and so I thought you . . . ?"

65

"I'm afraid I have another commitment," Miranda said firmly.

"You do? You couldn't possibly break it?"

"I don't see how I can, now."

"But I thought you, of all people . . . I mean . . ."

"Yes, Mrs. Boyer, I understand. And I'm sorry."

"I don't know who else to call," Mrs. Boyer said. "Can you think of anyone? You must know someone, some other elder . . . some other person?"

"I don't know anyone," Miranda said. "No one at all."

She said goodbye and replaced the receiver. She buttoned her coat, worked her gnarled fingers into the gloves, then crossed the rear porch and stepped outside.

The wind was blustery and very cold, but she didn't hurry. It would not do to hurry at a time like this. She walked at a steady, measured pace across the leaf-strewn yard to the barn.

The front half was mostly a dusty catchall storage area, as it had been when John was alive. On the right side was a cleared section just large enough for her car; the remaining floor space was packed with trunks, boxes, discarded appliances, gardening equipment, and the like. Some of the cartons had been there for so long Miranda no longer had any idea what they contained. She made her way along the passenger side of the car to the doorway in the center partition; opened it and passed through into John's workshop.

His last few woodworking projects, finished and unfinished, were bulky mounds under the dustcloths she had placed over them. His workbench, lathe, table saws, and such were also shrouded. The bench was where the coiled rope lay, but Miranda did not go in that direction. Nor did she glance up at the ceiling beam in the shadows above.

At the workshop's far end, more shadows crowded the alcove where John had kept his cot and tiny refrigerator. On those long ago summer nights when he had been deep into one of his projects, he had slept out here to avoid disturbing her. Now there was nothing inside the alcove, only the bare wood floor over packed earth.

Miranda knelt and raised the cunningly hidden hinged section. Underneath, the flowers she had placed there last week were already withered and crumbling, dust and petals scattered across the pair of old graves.

So many years since she'd found John and Moira together here that night. So many years since the strangest whim had seized her and she'd done what she felt she must—shot them both with one of John's handguns, quickly and efficiently, for no one should have to suffer when the time came. So many years since she had, in her supremely capable fashion, dug for each of them a final resting place and then, using the woodworking skills John had taught her, rebuilt the flooring to cover the graves.

No one had ever suspected. John Halliday had run off with his wife's beautiful younger sister—that was what everyone believed. Such a terrible tragedy for poor Miranda, they all said. But no one except her could know how terrible it really was to be left all alone with nobody to love except a little dog and fewer and fewer and fewer ways in which to atone for her sin.

It would be quite a shock when the citizens of Shady Grove learned the truth. And learn it they must; she had kept the secret too long and she could not carry it with her to her own grave—in the words of the poet Andrew Marvell, that "fine and private place." She had explained everything in the three-page letter; it would be her final act of atonement.

John and Moira knew all about the rope and the letter. Over and over she had told them that one day she must again do what she felt was necessary. Yet they were so reluctant to let her go. She could feel their reluctance now. Selfish. Even in death, they cared only for themselves.

"John," she said, "this is the proper day. Can't you understand how I feel?"

The wind mourned outside.

"Moira? We've hurt each other enough. Isn't it time we were together again?"

The last of the flowers suddenly trembled and broke apart. The earth seemed to tremble, too, as if there were stirrings within. It was only a draft caused by the wind, she knew it could be nothing else, yet it was as if they had caused it. As if they were beseeching and mocking her, saying quite clearly: "You can't leave us, Miranda. Who will tend to us once you're gone? Who will bring flowers and keep the weeds from growing up around us?

"*We* need you, Miranda. You know that, don't you?"

She did not argue; it never did any good to argue. She sighed and got slowly to her feet. "After all," she said, "I think I will not hang myself today."

She lowered the hinged section, thinking that she must buy fresh flowers to replace the withered ones because it was autumn and there were none left in the garden. But before she called the florist, she would ring up Mrs. Boyer and tell her she would be able to babysit tonight after all.

The Man Who Collected "The Shadow"

Mr. Theodore Conway was a nostalgist, a collector of memorabilia, a dweller in the uncomplicated days of his adolescence when radio, movie serials, and pulp magazines were the ruling forms of entertainment and super-heroes were the idols of American youth.

At forty-three, he resided alone in a modest apartment on Manhattan's Lower East Side, where he commuted daily by subway to his position of file clerk in the archives of Baylor, Baylor, Leeds and Wadsworth, a respected probate law firm. He was short and balding and very plump and very nondescript; he did not indulge in any of the vices, major or minor; he had no friends to speak of, and neither a wife nor, euphemistically or otherwise, a girlfriend. (In point of fact, Mr. Conway was that rarest of individuals, an adult male virgin.) He did not own a television set, did not attend the theater or movies. His one and only hobby, his single source of pleasure, his sole purpose in life, was the accumulation of nostalgia in general—and nostalgia pertaining to that most inimitable of all super-heroes, The Shadow, in particular.

Ah, The Shadow! Mr. Conway idolized Lamont Cranston, loved Margo Lane as he could never love any living woman. Nothing set his blood to racing quite so quickly as The Shadow on the scent of an evildoer, utilizing the Power that, as Cranston, he had learned in the Orient—the Power to cloud men's minds so that they could not see him. Nothing gave Mr. Conway more pleasure than listening to the haunting voice of Orson Welles, capturing The Shadow as no other had over the air; or reading Maxwell Grant's daring accounts in *The Shadow Magazine*; or paging through one of the starkly drawn Shadow comic books. Nothing filled him with as much delicious anticipation as the words spoken by his hero at the beginning of each radio adventure: *Who knows what evil lurks in the hearts of men? The Shadow knows* . . . and the eerie, bloodcurdling laugh that followed it. Nothing filled him with as much security as, when each case was closed, this ace among aces saying words of warning to criminals everywhere: *The weed of crime bears bitter fruit. Crime does not pay. The Shadow knows!*

Mr. Conway had begun collecting nostalgia in 1946, starting with a wide range of pulp magazines. (He now had well over ten thousand issues of *Wu Fang, G-8 and his Battle Aces, Black Mask, Weird Tales, Doc Savage*, and two hundred others.) Then he had gone on to comic books and comic strips, to premiums of every kind and description—decoders and secret compartment belts and message flashlights and spy rings and secret pens that wrote in invisible ink. In the 1970s he had begun to accumulate tapes of such radio shows as *Jack Armstrong, the All-American Boy* and *Buck Rogers in the 25th Century*. But while he amassed all of these eagerly, he pursued the mystique of The Shadow with a fervor that bordered on the fanatical.

He haunted secondhand bookshops and junk shops, pored over advertisements in newspapers and magazines and collectors' sheets, wrote letters, made telephone calls, spent every penny of his salary that did not go for bare essentials. And at long last he succeeded where no other nostalgist had even come close to succeeding. He accomplished a remarkable, an almost superhuman feat.

He collected the complete Shadow.

There was absolutely nothing produced about his hero—

not a written word, not a spoken sentence, not a drawing or gadget—that Mr. Conway did not own.

The final item, the one that had eluded him for so many years, came into his possession on a Saturday evening in late June. He had gone into a tenement area of Manhattan, near the East River, to purchase from a private individual a rare cartoon strip of *Terry and the Pirates*. With the strip carefully tucked into his coat pocket, he was on his way back to the subway when he chanced upon a small neighborhood book-shop in the basement of a crumbling brownstone. It was still open, and unfamiliar to him, and so he entered and began to browse. And on one of the cluttered tables at the rear—there it was.

The October 1931 issue of *The Shadow Magazine*.

Mr. Conway emitted a small, ecstatic cry. Caught up the magazine in trembling hands, stared at it with disbelieving eyes, opened it tenderly, read the contents page and the date, ran sweat-slick fingers over the rough, grainy pulp paper. Near-mint condition. Spine undamaged. Colors unfaded. And the price—

Fifty cents.

Fifty cents!

Tears of joy rolled unabashedly down Mr. Conway's cheeks as he carried this treasure to the elderly proprietor. The bookseller gave him a strange look, shrugged, and accepted two quarters from Mr. Conway without a word. Two quarters, fifty cents. And Mr. Conway had been prepared to pay *hundreds* . . .

As he went out into the gathering darkness—it was almost nine by this time—he could scarcely believe that he had finally done it, that he now possessed the total word, picture, and voice exploits of the most awesome master crime fighter of them all. His brain reeled. The Shadow was *his* now;

Lamont Cranston and Margo Lane (beautiful Margo!)—his, all his, his alone.

Instead of proceeding to the subway, Mr. Conway impulsively entered a small diner not far from the bookshop and ordered a cup of coffee. Then, once again, he opened the magazine. He had previously read a reprint of the novel by Maxwell Grant—*The Shadow Laughs!*—but that was not the same as reading the original, no indeed. He plunged into the story again, savoring each line, each page, the mounting suspense, the seemingly inescapable traps laid to eliminate The Shadow by archvillains Isaac Coffran and Birdie Crull, the smashing of their insidious counterfeiting plot: justice triumphant. *The weed of crime bears bitter fruit, crime does not pay . . .*

So engrossed was Mr. Conway that he lost all track of time. When at last he closed the magazine he was startled to note that except for the counterman, the diner was deserted. It had been nearly full when he entered. He looked at his wristwatch, and his mouth dropped open in amazement. Good heavens! It was past midnight!

Mr. Conway scrambled out of the booth and hurriedly left the diner. Outside, apprehension seized him. The streets were dark and deserted—ominous, forbidding.

He looked up and down without seeing any sign of life. It was four blocks to the nearest subway entrance—a short walk in daylight but now it was almost the dead of night. Mr. Conway shivered in the cool night breeze. He had never liked the night, its sounds and smells, its hidden dangers. There were stories in the papers every morning of muggers and thieves on the prowl . . .

He took a deep breath, summoning courage. Four blocks. Well, that really wasn't very far, only a matter of minutes if he walked swiftly. And swift was his pace as he started along the darkened sidewalk.

No cars passed; no one appeared on foot. The hollow echo of his footfalls were the only sounds. And yet Mr. Conway's heart was pounding wildly by the time he had gone two blocks.

He was halfway through the third block when he heard the muffled explosions.

He stopped, the hairs on his neck prickling, a tremor of fear coursing through him. There was an alley on his left; the reports had come from that direction. Gunshots? He was certain that was what they'd been—and even more certain that they meant danger, sudden death. *Run!* he thought. And yet, though he was poised for flight, he did not run. He peered into the alley, saw a thin light at its far end.

Run, run! But instead he entered the alley, moving slowly, feeling his way along. *What am I doing? I shouldn't be here!* But still he continued forward, approaching the narrow funnel of light. It came from inside a partly open door to the building on his right. Mr. Conway put out a hand and eased the door open wider, peered into what looked to be a warehouse. The thudding of his heart seemed as loud as a drum roll as he stepped over the threshold.

The source of the light was a glassed-in cubicle toward the middle of the warehouse. Shadowy shapes—crates of some kind—loomed toward the ceiling on either side. He advanced in hesitant, wary steps, seeing no sign of movement in the gloom around him. At last he reached the cubicle, stood in the light. A watchman's office. He stepped up close to look through the glass.

A cry rose in his throat when he saw the man lying motionless on the floor inside; he managed to stifle it. Blood stained the front of the man's khaki uniform jacket. He had been shot twice.

Dead, murdered! Get out of here, call the police!

Mr. Conway turned—and froze.

A hulking figure stood not three feet away, looking straight at him.

Mr. Conway's knees buckled; he had to put a hand against the glass to keep from collapsing. The murderer! His mind once again compelled him to run, run, but his legs would not obey. He could only stare back in horror at the hulking figure—at the pinched white face beneath a low-brimmed cloth cap, at rodentlike eyes and a cruel mouth, at the yawning muzzle of a revolver in one fist.

"No!" Mr. Conway cried then. "No, please, don't shoot!"

The man dropped into a furtive crouch, extending the pistol in front of him.

"Don't shoot!" Mr. Conway said again, putting up his hands.

Surprise, bewilderment, and a sudden trapped fear made a twisted mask of the man's face. "Who's that? Who's there?"

Mr. Conway opened his mouth, then closed it again. He could scarcely believe his ears. The man was standing not three feet away, looking right at him!

"I don't understand," Mr. Conway said before he could stop the words.

The murderer fired. The sudden report caused Mr. Conway to jump convulsively aside; the bullet came nowhere near him. He saw the gunman looking desperately from side to side, everywhere but at him—and in that instant he did understand, he knew.

"You can't *see* me," he said.

The gun discharged a second bullet, but Mr. Conway had already moved again. Far to one side of him a spider-webbed hole appeared in the glass wall of the cubicle. "Damn you!" the murderer screamed. "Where are you? *Where are you?*"

Mr. Conway remained standing there, clearly outlined in

the light, for a moment longer; then he stepped to where a board lay on the floor nearby, picked it up. Without hesitation, he advanced on the terrified man and then struck him on the side of the head; watched dispassionately as the other dropped unconscious to the floor.

Mr. Conway kicked the revolver away and stood over him. The police would have to be summoned, of course, but there was plenty of time for that now. A slow, grim smile stretched the corners of his mouth. Could it be that the remarkable collecting feat he had performed, his devotion and his passion, had stirred some supernatural force into granting him the Power that he now possessed? Well, no matter. His was not to question why; his was but to heed the plaintive cries of a world ridden with lawlessness.

A deep, chilling laugh suddenly swept through the warehouse. "The weed of crime bears bitter fruit!" a haunting, Wellesian voice shouted. "Crime does not pay!"

And The Shadow wrapped the cloak of night around himself and went out into the mean streets of the great metropolis . . .

Out of the Depths

He came tumbling out of the sea, dark and misshapen, like a being that was not human. A creature from the depths; or a jumbee, the evil spirit of West Indian superstition. Fanciful thoughts, and Shea was not a fanciful woman. But on this strange, wild night nothing seemed real or explicable.

At first, with the moon hidden behind the running scud of clouds, she'd seen him as a blob of flotsam on a breaking wave. The squall earlier had left the sea rough and the swells out toward the reef were high, their crests stripped of spume by the wind. The angry surf threw him onto the strip of beach, dragged him back again; another wave flung him up a little farther. The moon reappeared then, bathing sea and beach and rocks in the kind of frost-white shine you found only in the Caribbean. Not flotsam—something alive. She saw his arms extend, splayed fingers dig into the sand to hold himself against the backward pull of the sea. Saw him raise a smallish head above a massive, deformed torso, then squirm weakly toward the nearest jut of rock. Another wave shoved him the last few feet. He clung to the rock, lying motionless with the surf foaming around him.

Out of the depths, she thought.

The irony made her shiver, draw the collar of her coat more tightly around her neck. She lifted her gaze again to the rocky peninsula farther south. Windflaw Point, where the undertow off its tiny beach was the most treacherous on the island. It had taken her almost an hour to marshal her courage to the point where she was ready—almost ready—

to walk out there and into the ocean. *Into* the depths. Now . . .

Massive clouds sealed off the moon again. In the heavy darkness Shea could just make him out, still lying motionless on the fine coral sand. Unconscious? Dead? I ought to go down there, she thought. But she could not seem to lift herself out of the chair.

After several minutes he moved again: dark shape rising to hands and knees, then trying to stand. Three tries before he was able to keep his legs from collapsing under him. He stood swaying, as if gathering strength; finally staggered onto the path that led up through rocks and sea grape. Toward the house. Toward her.

On another night she would have felt any number of emotions by this time: surprise, bewilderment, curiosity, concern. But not on this night. There was a numbness in her mind, like the numbness in her body from the cold wind. It was as if she were dreaming, sitting there on the open terrace—as if she'd fallen asleep hours ago, before the clouds began to pile up at sunset and the sky turned the color of a blood bruise.

A new storm was making up. Hammering northern this time, from the look of the sky. The wind had shifted, coming out of the northeast now; the clouds were bloated and simmering in that direction and the air had a charged quality. Unless the wind shifted again soon, the rest of the night would be even wilder.

Briefly the clouds released the moon. In its white glare she saw him plodding closer, limping, almost dragging his left leg. A man, of course—just a man. And not deformed: what had made him seem that way was the life jacket fastened around his upper body. She remembered the lights of a freighter or tanker she had seen passing on the horizon just after nightfall, ahead of the squall. Had he gone overboard from that somehow?

He had reached the garden, was making his way past the flamboyant trees and the thick clusters of frangipani. Heading toward the garden door and the kitchen: she'd left the lights on in there and the jalousies open. It was the lights that had drawn him here, like a beacon that could be seen a long distance out to sea.

A good thing she'd left them on or not? She didn't want him here, a cast-up stranger, hurt and needing attention—not on this night, not when she'd been so close to making the walk to Windflaw Point. But neither could she refuse him access or help. John would have, if he'd been drunk and in the wrong mood. Not her. It was not in her nature to be cruel to anyone, except perhaps herself.

Abruptly Shea pushed herself out of the chair. He hadn't seen her sitting in the restless shadows, and he didn't see her now as she moved back across the terrace to the sliding glass doors to her bedroom. Or at least if he did see her, he didn't stop or call out to her. She hurried through the darkened bedroom, down the hall, and into the kitchen. She was halfway to the garden door when he began pounding on it.

She unlocked and opened the door without hesitation. He was propped against the stucco wall, arms hanging and body slumped with exhaustion. Big and youngish, that was her first impression. She couldn't see his face clearly.

"Need some help," he said in a thick, strained voice. "Been in the water . . . washed up on your beach. . . ."

"I know, I saw you from the terrace. Come inside."

"Better get a towel first. Coral ripped a gash in my foot . . . blood all over your floor."

"All right. I'll have to close the door. The wind. . . ."

"Go ahead."

She shut the door and went to fetch a towel, a blanket, and the first-aid kit. On the way back to the kitchen she turned the heat up several degrees. When she opened up to him again she saw that he'd shed the life jacket. His clothing was minimal: plaid wool shirt, denim trousers, canvas shoes, all nicked and torn by coral. Around his waist was a pouch-type waterproof belt, like a workman's utility belt. One of the pouches bulged slightly.

She gave him the towel, and when he had it wrapped around his left foot he hobbled inside. She took his arm, let him lean on her as she guided him to the kitchen table. His flesh was cold, sea-puckered; the touch of it made her feel a tremor of revulsion. It was like touching the skin of a dead man.

When he sank heavily onto one of the chairs, she dragged another chair over and lifted his injured leg onto it. He stripped off what was left of his shirt, swaddled himself in the blanket. His teeth were chattering.

The coffeemaker drew her; she poured two of the big mugs full. There was always hot coffee ready and waiting, no matter what the hour—she made sure of that. She drank too much coffee, much too much, but it was better than drinking what John usually drank. If she—

"You mind sweetening that?"

She half-turned. "Sugar?"

"Liquor. Rum, if you have it."

"Jamaican rum." That was what John drank.

"Best there is. Fine."

She took down an open bottle, carried it and the mugs to the table, and watched while he spiked the coffee, drank, then poured more rum and drank again. Color came back into his stubbled cheeks. He used part of the blanket to rough-dry his hair.

He was a little older than she, early thirties, and in good physical condition: broad chest and shoulders, muscle-knotted arms. Sandy hair cropped short, thick sandy brows, a long-chinned face burned dark from exposure to the sun. The face was all right, might have been attractive except for the eyes. They were a bright off-blue color, shielded by lids that seemed perpetually lowered like flags at halfmast, and they didn't blink much. When the eyes lifted to meet and hold hers something in them made her look away.

"I'll see what I can do for your foot."

"Thanks. Hurts like hell."

The towel was already soaking through. Shea unwrapped it carefully, revealing a deep gash across the instep just above the tongue of his shoe. She got the shoe and sock off. More blood welled out of the cut.

"It doesn't look good. You may need a doctor—"

"No," he said, "no doctor."

"It'll take stitches to close properly."

"Just clean and bandage it, okay?"

She spilled iodine onto a gauze pad, swabbed at the gash as gently as she could. The sharp sting made him suck in his breath, but he didn't flinch or utter another sound. She laid a second piece of iodined gauze over the wound and began to wind tape tightly around his foot to hold the skin flaps together.

He said, "My name's Tanner. Harry Tanner."

"Shea Clifford."

"Shea. That short for something?"

"It's a family name."

"Pretty."

"Thank you."

"So are you," he said. "Real pretty with your hair all wind-blown like that."

She glanced up at him. He was smiling at her. Not a leer, just a weary smile, but it wasn't a good kind of smile. It had a predatory look, like the teeth-baring stretch of a wolf's jowls.

"No offense," he said.

"None taken." She lowered her gaze, watched her hands wind and tear tape. Her mind still felt numb. "What happened to you? Why were you in the water?"

"That damn squall a few hours ago. Came up so fast I didn't have time to get my genoa down. Wave as big as a house knocked poor little *Wanderer* into a full broach. I got thrown clear when she went over or I'd have sunk with her."

"Were you sailing alone?"

"All alone."

"Single-hander? Or just on a weekend lark?"

"Single-hander. You know boats, I see."

"Yes. Fairly well."

"Well, I'm a sea tramp," Tanner said. "Ten years of island-hopping and this is the first time I ever got caught unprepared."

"It happens. What kind of craft was *Wanderer*?"

"Bugeye ketch. Thirty-nine feet."

"Shame to lose a boat like that."

He shrugged. "She was insured."

"How far out were you?"

"Five or six miles. Hell of a long swim in a choppy sea."

"You're lucky the squall passed as quickly as it did."

"Lucky I was wearing my life jacket, too," Tanner said. "And lucky you stay up late with your lights on. If it weren't for the lights I probably wouldn't have made shore at all."

Shea nodded. She tore off the last piece of tape and then began putting the first-aid supplies away in the kit.

Tanner said, "I didn't see any other lights. This house the only one out here?"

"The only one on this side of the bay, yes."

"No close neighbors?"

"Three houses on the east shore, not far away."

"You live here alone?"

"With my husband."

"But he's not here now."

"Not now. He'll be home soon."

"That so? Where is he?"

"In Merrywing, the town on the far side of the island. He went out to dinner with friends."

"While you stayed home."

"I wasn't feeling well earlier."

"Merrywing. Salt Cay?"

"That's right."

"British-owned, isn't it?"

"Yes. You've never been here before?"

"Not my kind of place. Too small, too quiet, too rich. I prefer the livelier islands—St. Thomas, Nassau, Jamaica."

"St. Thomas isn't far from here," Shea said. "Is that where you were heading?"

"More or less. This husband of yours—how big is he?"

". . . Big?"

"Big enough so his clothes would fit me?"

"Oh," she said, "yes. About your size."

"Think he'd mind if you let me have a pair of his pants and a shirt and some underwear? Wet things of mine are giving me a chill."

"No, of course not. I'll get them from his room."

She went to John's bedroom. The smells of his cologne and pipe tobacco were strong in there; they made her faintly nauseous. In haste she dragged a pair of white linen trousers and a pullover off hangers in his closet, turned toward the dresser as she came out. And stopped in midstride.

Tanner stood in the open doorway, leaning against the jamb, his half-lidded eyes fixed on her.

"*His* room," he said. "Right."

"Why did you follow me?"

"Felt like it. So you don't sleep with him."

"Why should that concern you?"

"I'm naturally curious. How come? I mean, how come you and your husband don't share a bed?"

"Our sleeping arrangements are none of your business."

"Probably not. Your idea or his?"

"What?"

"Separate bedrooms. Your idea or his?"

"Mine, if you must know."

"Maybe he snores, huh?"

She didn't say anything.

"How long since you kicked him out of your bed?"

"I didn't kick him out. It wasn't like that."

"Sure it was. I can see it in your face."

"My private affairs—"

"—are none of my business. I know. But I also know the signs of a bad marriage when I see them. A bad marriage and an unhappy woman. Can't tell me you're not unhappy."

"All right," she said.

"So why don't you divorce him? Money?"

"Money has nothing to do with it."

"Money has something to do with everything."

"It isn't money."

"He have something on you?"

"No."

"Then why not just dump him?"

You're not going to divorce me, Shea. Not you, not like the others. I'll see you dead first. I mean it, Shea. You're mine and you'll stay mine until I decide I don't want you anymore. . . .

She said flatly, "I'm not going to talk about my marriage to you. I don't know you."

"We can fix that. I'm an easy guy to know."

She moved ahead to the dresser, found underwear and socks, put them on the bed with the trousers and pullover. "You can change in here," she said, and started for the doorway.

Tanner didn't move.

"I said—"

"I heard you, Shea."

"Mrs. Clifford."

"Clifford," he said. Then he smiled, the same wolfish lip-stretch he'd shown her in the kitchen. "Sure—Clifford. Your husband's name wouldn't be John, would it? John Clifford?"

She was silent.

"I'll bet it is. John Clifford, Clifford Yacht Designs. One of the best marine architects in Miami. Fancy motor sailers and racing yawls."

She still said nothing.

"House in Miami Beach, another on Salt Cay—this house. And you're his latest wife. Which is it, number three or number four?"

Between her teeth she said, "Three."

"He must be what, fifty now? And worth millions. Don't tell me money's not why you married him."

"I won't tell you anything."

But his wealth *wasn't* why she'd married him. He had been kind and attentive to her at first. And she'd been lonely after the bitter breakup with Neal. John had opened up a whole new, exciting world to her: travel to exotic places, sailing, the company of interesting and famous people. She hadn't loved him, but she had been fond of him; and she'd convinced her-self she would learn to love him in time. Instead, when he revealed his dark side to her, she had learned to hate him.

Tanner said, "Didn't one of his other wives divorce him for knocking her around when he was drunk? Seems I remember reading something like that in the Miami papers a few years back. That why you're unhappy, Shea? He knock you around when he's drinking?"

Without answering, Shea pushed past him into the hallway. He didn't try to stop her. In the kitchen again she poured yet another cup of coffee and sat down with it. Even with her coat on and the furnace turned up, she was still cold. The heat from the mug failed to warm her hands.

She knew she ought to be afraid of Harry Tanner. But all she felt inside was a deep weariness. An image of Windflaw Point, the tiny beach with its treacherous undertow, flashed across the screen of her mind—and was gone again just as swiftly. Her courage, or maybe her cowardice, was gone too. She was no longer capable of walking out to the point, letting the sea have her. Not tonight and probably not ever again.

She sat listening to the wind clamor outside. It moaned in the twisted branches of the banyan tree; scraped palm fronds against the roof tiles. Through the open window jalousies she could smell ozone mixed with the sweet fragrances of white ginger blooms. The new storm would be here soon in all its fury.

The wind kept her from hearing Tanner reenter the kitchen. She sensed his presence, looked up, and saw him standing there with his eyes on her like probes. He'd put on all of John's clothing and found a pair of Reeboks for his feet. In his left hand he held the waterproof belt that had been strapped around his waist.

"Shirt's a little snug," he said, "but a pretty good fit otherwise. Your husband's got nice taste."

Shea didn't answer.

"In clothing, in houses, and in women."

She sipped her coffee, not looking at him.

Tanner limped around the table and sat down across from her. When he laid the belt next to the bottle of rum, the pouch that bulged made a thunking sound. "Boats too," he said. "I'll bet he keeps his best designs for himself; he's the kind that would. Am I right, Shea?"

"Yes."

"How many boats does he own?"

"Two."

"One's bound to be big. Oceangoing yacht?"

"Seventy-foot custom schooner."

"What's her name?"

"*Moneybags*."

Tanner laughed. "Some sense of humor."

"If you say so."

"Where does he keep her? Here or Miami?"

"Miami."

"She there now?"

"Yes."

"And the other boat? That one berthed here?"

"The harbor at Merrywing."

"What kind is she?"

"A sloop," Shea said. "*Carib Princess*."

"How big?"

"Thirty-two feet."

"She been back and forth across the Stream?"

"Several times, in good weather."

"With you at the helm?"

"No."

"You ever take her out by yourself?"

"No. He wouldn't allow it."

"But you can handle her, right? You said you know boats.

You can pilot that little sloop without any trouble?"

"Why do you want to know that? Why are you asking so many questions about John's boats?"

"John's boats, John's houses, John's third wife." Tanner laughed again, just a bark this time. The wolfish smile pulled his mouth out of shape. "Are you afraid of me, Shea?"

"No."

"Not even a little?"

"Why? Should I be?"

"What do you think?"

"I'm not afraid of you," she said.

"Then how come you lied to me?"

"Lied? About what?"

"Your husband. Old John Clifford."

"I don't know what you mean."

"You said he'd be home soon. But he won't be. He's not in town with friends, he's not even on the island."

She stared silently at the steam rising from her cup. Her fingers felt cramped, as if she might be losing circulation in them.

"Well, Shea? That's the truth, isn't it."

"Yes. That's the truth."

"Where is he? Miami?"

She nodded.

"Went there on business and left you all by your lonesome."

"It isn't the first time."

"Might be the last, though." Tanner reached for the rum bottle, poured some of the dark liquid into his mug, drank, and then smacked his lips. "You want a shot of this?"

"No."

"Loosen you up a little."

"I don't need loosening up."

"You might after I tell you the truth about Harry Tanner."

"Does that mean you lied to me too?"

"I'm afraid so. But you 'fessed up and now it's my turn."

In the blackness outside the wind gusted sharply, banging a loose shutter somewhere at the front of the house. Rain began to pelt down with open-faucet suddenness.

"Listen to that," Tanner said. "Sounds like we're in for a big blow, this time."

"What did you lie about?"

"Well, let's see. For starters, about how I came to be in the water tonight. My bugeye ketch didn't sink in the squall. No, *Wanderer*'s tied up at a dock in Charlotte Amalie."

She sat stiffly, waiting.

"Boat I was on didn't sink either," Tanner said. "At least as far as I know it didn't. I jumped overboard. Not long after the squall hit us."

There was still nothing for her to say.

"If I hadn't gone overboard, the two guys I was with would've shot me dead. They tried to shoot me in the water but the ketch was pitching like crazy and they couldn't see me in the dark and the rain. I guess they figured I'd drown even with a life jacket on. Or the sharks or barracuda would get me."

Still nothing.

"We had a disagreement over money. That's what most things come down to these days—money. They thought I cheated them out of twenty thousand dollars down in Jamaica, and they were right, I did. They both put guns on me before I could do anything and I thought I was a dead man. The squall saved my bacon. Big swell almost broached us, knocked us all off our feet. I managed to scramble up the companionway and go over the side before they recovered."

The hard beat of the rain stopped as suddenly as it had

begun. Momentary lull: the full brunt of the storm was minutes away yet.

"I'm not a single-hander," he said, "not a sea tramp. That's another thing I lied about. Ask me what it is I really am, Shea. Ask me how I make my living."

"I don't have to ask."

"No? Think you know?"

"Smuggling. You're a smuggler."

"That's right. Smart lady."

"Drugs, I suppose."

"Drugs, weapons, liquor, the wretched poor yearning to breathe free without benefit of a green card. You name it, I've handled it. Hell, smuggling's a tradition in these waters. Men have been doing it for three hundred years, since the days of the Spanish Main." He laughed. "A modern freebooter, that's what I am. Tanner the Pirate. Yo ho ho and a bottle of rum."

"Why are you telling me all this?"

"Why not? Don't you find it interesting?"

"No."

"Okay, I'll give it to you straight. I've got a problem—a big problem. I jumped off that ketch tonight with one thing besides the clothes on my back, and it wasn't money." He pulled the waterproof belt to him, unsnapped the pouch that bulged, and showed her what was inside. "Just this."

Her gaze registered the weapon—automatic, large caliber, lightweight frame—and slid away. She was not surprised; she had known there was a gun in the pouch when it made the thunking sound.

Tanner set it on the table within easy reach. "My two partners got my share of a hundred thousand from the Jamaica run. I might be able to get it back from them and I might not; they're a couple of hard cases and I'm not sure it's worth the risk. But I can't do anything until I quit this island. And I can't leave the usual ways because my money and my passport are both on that damn ketch. You see my dilemma, Shea?"

"I see it."

"Sure you do. You're a smart lady, like I said. What else do you see? The solution?"

She shook her head.

"Well, I've got a dandy." The predatory grin again. "You know, this really is turning into my lucky night. I couldn't have washed up in a better spot if I'd planned it. John Clifford's house, John Clifford's smart and pretty wife. And not far away, John Clifford's little sloop, the *Carib Princess*."

The rain came again, wind-driven with enough force to rattle the windows. Spray blew in through the screens behind the open jalousies. Shea made no move to get up and close the glass. Tanner didn't even seem to notice the moisture.

"Here's what we're going to do," he said. "At dawn we'll drive in to the harbor. You do have a car here? Sure you do; he wouldn't leave you isolated without wheels. Once we get there we go on-board the sloop and you take her out. If anybody you know sees us and says anything, you tell them I'm a friend or relative and John said it was okay for us to go for a sail without him."

She asked dully, "Then what?"

"Once we're out to sea? I'm not going to kill you and dump your body overboard, if that's worrying you. The only thing that's going to happen is we sail the *Carib Princess* across the Stream to Florida. A little place I know on the west coast up near Pavilion Key where you can sneak a boat in at night and keep her hidden for as long as you need to."

"And then?"

"Then I call your husband and we do some business. How

90

much do you think he'll pay to get his wife and his sloop back safe and sound? Five hundred thousand? As much as a million?"

"My God," she said. "You're crazy."

"Like a fox."

"You couldn't get away with it. You *can't*."

"I figure I can. You think he won't pay because the marriage is on the rocks? You're wrong, Shea. He'll pay, all right. He's the kind that can't stand losing anything that belongs to him, wife or boat, and sure as hell not both at once. Plus he's had enough bad publicity; ignoring a ransom demand would hurt his image and his business and I'll make damned sure he knows it."

She shook her head again—a limp, rag-doll wobbling, as if it were coming loose from the stem of her neck.

"Don't look so miserable," Tanner said cheerfully. "I'm not such a bad guy when you get to know me, and there'll be plenty of time for us to get acquainted. And when old John pays off, I'll leave you with the sloop and you can sail her back to Miami. Okay? Give you my word on that."

He was lying: his word was worthless. He'd told her his name, the name of his ketch and where it was berthed; he wouldn't leave her alive to identify him. Not on the Florida coast. Not even here.

Automatically Shea picked up her mug, tilted it to her mouth. Dregs. Empty. She pushed back her chair, crossed to the counter, and poured the mug full again. Tanner sat relaxed, smiling, pleased with himself. The rising steam from the coffee formed a screen between them, so that she saw him as blurred, distorted. Not quite human, the way he had first seemed to her when he came out of the sea earlier.

Jumbee, she thought. Smiling evil.

The gale outside flung sheets of water at the house. The

loose shutter chattered like a jackhammer until the wind slackened again.

Tanner said, "Going to be a long wet night." He made a noisy yawning sound. "Where do you sleep, Shea?"

The question sent a spasm through her body.

"Your bedroom—where is it?"

Oh God. "Why?"

"I told you, it's going to be a long night. And I'm tired and my foot hurts and I want to lie down. But I don't want to lie down alone. We might as well start getting to know each other the best way there is."

No, she thought. No, no, no.

"Well, Shea? Lead the way."

No, she thought again. But her legs worked as if with a will of their own, carried her back to the table. Tanner sat forward as she drew abreast of him, started to lift himself out of the chair.

She threw the mug of hot coffee into his face.

She hadn't planned to do it, acted without thinking; it was almost as much of a surprise to her as it was to him. He yelled and pawed at his eyes, his body jerking so violently that both he and the chair toppled over sideways. Shea swept the automatic off the table and backed away with it extended at arm's length.

Tanner kicked the chair away and scrambled unsteadily to his feet. Bright red splotches stained his cheeks where the coffee had scalded him; his eyes were murderous. He took a step toward her, stopped when he realized she was pointing his own weapon at him. She watched him struggle to regain control of himself and the situation.

"You shouldn't have done that, Shea."

"Stay where you are."

"That gun isn't loaded."

"It's loaded. I know guns too."

"You won't shoot me." He took another step.

"I will. Don't come any closer."

"No you won't. You're not the type. I can pull the trigger on a person real easy. Have, more than once." Another step. "But not you. You don't have what it takes."

"Please don't make me shoot you. Please, please don't."

"See? You won't do it because you can't."

"Please."

"You won't shoot me, Shea."

On another night, any other night, he would have been right. But on this night—

He lunged at her.

And she shot him.

The impact of the high-caliber bullet brought him up short, as if he had walked into an invisible wall. A look of astonishment spread over his face. He took one last convulsive step before his hands came up to clutch at his chest and his knees buckled.

Shea didn't see him fall; she turned away. And the hue and the cry of the storm kept her from hearing him hit the floor. When she looked again, after several seconds, he lay face down and unmoving on the tiles. She did not have to go any closer to tell that he was dead.

There was a hollow queasiness in her stomach. Otherwise she felt nothing. She turned again, and there was a blank space of time, and then she found herself sitting on one of the chairs in the living room. She would have wept then but she had no tears. She had cried herself dry on the terrace.

After a while she became aware that she still gripped Tanner's automatic. She set it down on an end table; hesitated, then picked it up again. The numbness was finally leaving her mind, a swift release that brought her thoughts into sharpening focus. When the wind and rain lulled again she stood, walked slowly down the hall to her bedroom. She steeled herself as she opened the door and turned on the lights.

From where he lay sprawled across the bed, John's sightless eyes stared up at her. The stain of blood on his bare chest, drying now, gleamed darkly in the lamp glow.

Wild night, mad night.

She hadn't been through hell just once, she'd been through it twice. First in here and then in the kitchen.

But she hadn't shot John. She hadn't. He'd come home at nine, already drunk, and tried to make love to her, and when she denied him he'd slapped her, kept slapping her. After three long hellish years she couldn't take it anymore, not anymore. She'd managed to get the revolver out of her nightstand drawer . . . not to shoot him, just as a threat to make him leave her alone. But he'd lunged at her, in almost the same way Tanner had, and they'd struggled, and the gun had gone off. And John Clifford was dead.

She had started to call the police. Hadn't because she knew they would not believe it was an accident. John was well liked and highly respected on Salt Cay; his public image was untarnished and no one, not even his close friends, believed his second wife's divorce claim or that he could ever mistreat anyone. She had never really been accepted here—some of the cattier rich women thought she was a gold digger—and she had no friends of her own in whom she could confide. John had seen to that. There were no marks on her body to prove his abuse, either; he'd always been very careful not to leave marks.

The island police would surely have claimed she'd killed him in cold blood. She'd have been arrested and tried and convicted and put in a prison much worse than the one in which she had lived the past three years. The prospect of that was unbearable. It was what had driven her out onto the terrace, to sit and think about the undertow at Windflaw Point. The sea, in those moments, had seemed her only way out.

Now there was another way.

Her revolver lay on the floor where it had fallen. John had given it to her when they were first married, because he was away so much; and he had taught her how to use it. It was one of three handguns he'd bought illegally in Miami.

Shea bent to pick it up. With a corner of the bedsheet she wiped the grip carefully, then did the same to Tanner's automatic. That gun too, she was certain, would not be registered anywhere.

Wearily she put the automatic in John's hand, closing his fingers around it. Then she retreated to the kitchen and knelt to place the revolver in Tanner's hand. The first-aid kit was still on the table; she would use it once more, when she finished talking to the chief constable in Merrywing.

We tried to help Tanner, John and I, she would tell him. And he repaid our kindness by attempting to rob us at gunpoint. John told him we kept money in our bedroom; he took the gun out of the nightstand before I could stop him. They shot each other. John died instantly, but Tanner didn't believe his wound was as serious as it was. He made me bandage it and then kept me in the kitchen, threatening to kill me too. I managed to catch him off guard and throw coffee in his face. When he tried to come after me the strain aggravated his wound and he collapsed and died.

If this were Miami, or one of the larger Caribbean islands, she could not hope to get away with such a story. But here the native constabulary was unsophisticated and inexperienced because there was so little crime on Salt Cay. They were much more likely to overlook the fact that John had been shot two and a half hours before Harry Tanner. Much more likely, too, to credit a double homicide involving a stranger, particularly when they investigated Tanner's background, than the accidental shooting of a respected resident who had been abusing his wife. Yes, she might just get away with it. If there was any justice left for her in this world, she would—and one day she'd leave Salt Cay a free woman again.

Out of the depths, she thought as she picked up the phone. Out of the depths. . . .

Bank Job

I was standing beside the tellers' cages, in the railed-off section where the branch manager's desk was located, when the knocking began on the bank's rear door.

Frowning, I looked over in that direction. Now, who the devil could that be? It was four o'clock and the Fairfield branch of the Midland National Bank had been closed for an hour; it seemed unlikely that a customer would arrive at this late time.

The knocking continued—a rather curious sort of summons, I thought. It was both urgent and hesitant, alternately loud and soft in an odd spasmodic way. I glanced a bit uneasily at the suitcase on the floor beside the desk. But I could not just ignore the rapping. Judging from its insistence, whoever it was seemed to know that the bank was still occupied.

I went out through the grate in the rail divider and walked slowly down the short corridor to the door. The shade was drawn over the glass there—I had drawn it myself earlier and I could not see out into the private parking area at the rear. The knocking, I realized as I stepped up to the door, was coming from down low on the wood panel, beneath the glass. A child? Still frowning, I drew back the edge of the shade and peered out.

The person out there was a man, not a child—a medium-sized man wearing a mustache, modishly styled hair, and a business suit and tie. He was down on one knee, with his right hand stretched out to the door; his left hand was pressed against the side of his head, and his temple and the tips of his fingers were stained with what appeared to be blood.

He saw me looking out at about the same time I saw him. We blinked at each other. He made an effort to rise, sank back onto his knee again, and said in a pained voice that barely carried through the door, "Accident . . . over in the driveway . . . I need a doctor."

I peered past him. As much of the parking area as I could see was deserted, but from my vantagepoint I could not make out the driveway on the south side of the bank. I hesitated, but when the man said plaintively, "Please . . . I need help," I reacted on impulse: I reached down, unlocked the door, and started to pull it open.

The man came upright in one fluid motion, drove a shoulder against the door, and crowded inside. The door edge cracked into my forehead and threw me backward, off-balance. My vision blurred for a moment, and when it cleared and I had my equilibrium again, I was looking not at one man but at two.

I was also looking at a gun, held competently in the hand of the first man.

The second one, who seemed to have materialized out of nowhere, closed and re-locked the door. Then he too produced a handgun and pointed it at me. He looked enough like the first man to be his brother—medium-sized, mustache, modishly styled hair, business suit, and tie. The only appreciable difference between them was that One was wearing a blue shirt and Two a white shirt.

I stared at them incredulously. "Who are you? What do you want?"

"Unnecessary questions," One said. He had a soft, well modulated voice, calm and reasonable. "It should be obvious who we are and what we want."

"My God," I said, "bank robbers."

"Bingo," Two said. His voice was scratchy, like sand rubbing on glass.

One took a handkerchief from his coat pocket and wiped the blood—or whatever the crimson stuff was—off his fingers and his temple. I realized as he did so that his mustache and hair, and those of the other man, were of the theatrical makeup variety.

"You just do what you're told," One said, "and everything will be fine. Turn around, walk up the hall."

I did that. By the time I stopped again in front of the rail divider, the incredulity had vanished and I had regained my composure. I turned once more to face them.

"I'm afraid you're going to be disappointed," I said.

"Is that right?" One said. "Why?"

"You're not going to be able to rob this bank."

"Why aren't we?"

"Because all the money has been put inside the vault for the weekend," I said. "And I've already set the time locks; the vault doors can't be opened by hand and the time locks won't release until nine o'clock Monday morning."

They exchanged a look. Their faces were expressionless, but their eyes, I saw, were narrowed and cold. One said to Two, "Check out the tellers' cages."

Two nodded and hurried through the divider gate.

One looked at me again. "What's your name?"

"Luther Baysinger," I said.

"You do what here, Luther?"

"I'm the Fairfield branch manager."

"You lock up the money this early every Friday?"

"Yes."

"How come you don't stay open until six o'clock?"

I gestured at the cramped old-fashioned room. "We're a small branch bank in a rural community," I said. "We do a limited business; there has been no need for us to expand our hours."

"Where're the other employees now?"

"I gave them permission to leave early for the weekend."

From inside the second of the two tellers' cages Two called, "Cash drawers are empty."

One said to me, "Let's go back to the vault."

I pivoted immediately, stepped through the gate, entered the cages, and led the two of them down the walkway to the outer vault door. One examined it, tugged on the wheel. When it failed to yield he turned back to me.

"No way to open this door before Monday morning?"

"None at all."

"You're *sure* of that?"

"Of course I'm sure. As I told you, I've set the time locks here, and on the door to the inner vault as well. The inner vault is where all the bank's assets are kept."

Two said, "Damn. I knew we should have waited when we saw the place close up. Now what do we do?"

One ignored him. "How much is in that inner vault?" he asked me. "Round numbers."

"A few thousand, that's all," I said carefully.

"Come on, Luther. How much is in there?"

His voice was still calm and reasonable, but he managed nonetheless to imply a threat to the words. If I continued to lie to him, he was saying tacitly, he would do unpleasant things to me.

I sighed. "Around twenty thousand," I said. "We have no need for more than that on hand. We're—"

"I know," One said, "'you're a small branch bank in a rural community. How many other people work here?"

"Just two."

"Both tellers?"

"Yes."

"What time do they come in on Monday morning?"

"Nine o'clock."

"Just when the vault locks release."

"Yes. But—"

"Suppose you were to call up those two tellers and tell them to come in at nine-thirty on Monday, instead of nine o'clock. Make up some kind of excuse. They wouldn't question that, would they?"

It came to me then, all too clearly, what he was getting at. A coldness settled on my neck and melted down along my back. "It won't work," I said.

He raised an eyebrow. "What won't work?"

"Kidnapping me and holding me hostage for the weekend."

"No? Why not?"

"The tellers *would* know something was wrong if I asked them to come in late on Monday."

"I doubt that."

"Besides," I lied, "I have a wife, three children, and a mother-in-law living in my house. You couldn't control all of them for an entire weekend."

"So we won't take you to your house. We'll take you somewhere else and have you call your family and tell them you've been called out of town unexpectedly."

"They wouldn't believe it."

"I think they would. Look, Luther, we don't want to hurt you. All we're interested in is that twenty thousand. We're a little short of cash right now; we need operating capital." He shrugged and looked at Two. "How about it?"

"Sure," Two said. "Okay by me."

"Let's go out front again, Luther."

A bit numbly I led them away from the vault. When we passed out of the tellers' cages, my eyes went to the suitcase beside the desk and lingered on it for a couple of seconds. I pulled my gaze away then—but not soon enough.

One said, "Hold it right there."

I stopped, half-turning, and when I saw him looking past me at the suitcase I grimaced.

One noticed that, too. "Planning a trip somewhere?" he asked.

"Ah . . . yes," I said. "A trip, yes. To the state capital—a bankers' convention. I'm expected there tonight and if I don't show up people will know something is wrong—"

"Nuts," One said. He glanced at Two. "Take a look inside that suitcase."

"Wait," I said, "I—"

"Shut up, Luther."

I shut up and watched Two lift the suitcase to the top of the desk, next to the nameplate there that read *Luther Baysinger, Branch Manager*. He snapped open the catches and swung up the lid.

Surprise registered on his face. "Hey," he said, "money. It's filled with *money*."

One stepped away from me and went over to stand beside Two, who was rifling through the packets of currency inside the suitcase. A moment later Two hesitated, then said, "What the hell?" and lifted out my .22 Colt Woodsman, which was also inside the case.

Both of them looked at me. I stared back defiantly. For several seconds it was very quiet in there; then, because there was nothing else to be done, I lowered my gaze and leaned against the divider.

"All right," I said, "the masquerade is over."

One said, "Masquerade? What's that supposed to mean, Luther?"

"My name isn't Luther," I said.

"What?"

"The real Luther Baysinger is locked inside the vault."

"What?"

"Along with both tellers."

Two said it this time, "What?"

"There's around eight thousand dollars in the suitcase," I said. "I cleaned it out of the cash room in the outer vault not long before you showed up."

"What the hell are you telling us?" One said. "Are you saying you're—"

"The same thing you are, that's right. I'm a bank robber."

They looked at each other. Both of them appeared confused now, no longer quite so sure of themselves.

One said, "I don't believe it."

I shrugged. "It's the truth. We both seem to have picked the same day to knock over the same bank, only I got here first. I've been casing this place for a week; I doubt if you cased it at all. A spur-of-the-moment job, am I right?"

"Hell," Two said to One, "he *is* right. We only just—"

"Be quiet," One said, "let me think." He gave me a long, searching look. "What's your name?"

"John Smith."

"Yeah, sure."

"Look," I said, "I'm not going to give you my right name. Why should I? You're not going to tell me yours."

One gestured to Two. "Frisk him," he said. "See if he's carrying any identification."

Two came over to me and ran his hands over my clothing, checked inside all the pockets of my suit. "No wallet," he said.

"Of course not," I said. "I'm a professional, same as you are. I'm not stupid enough to carry identification on a job."

Two went back to where One was standing and they held a whispered conference, giving me sidewise looks all the while.

At the end of two minutes, One faced me again.

"Let's get this straight," he said. "When did you come in here?"

"Just before three o'clock."

"And then what?"

"I waited until I was the last person in the place except for Baysinger and the two tellers. Then I threw down on them with the Woodsman. The inner vault was already time-locked, so I cleaned out the tellers' drawers and the cash room, and locked them in the outer vault."

"All of that took you an hour, huh?"

"Not quite. It was almost quarter past three before the last customer left, and I spent some time talking to Baysinger about the inner vault before I was convinced he couldn't open it. I was just getting ready to leave when you got here." I gave him a rueful smile. "It was a damned foolish move, going to the door without the gun and then opening up for you. But you caught me off-guard. That accident ploy is pretty clever."

"It's a good thing for you that you didn't have the gun," Two said. "You'd be dead now."

"Or you'd be," I said.

We exchanged more silent stares.

"Anyhow," I said at length, "I thought I could bluff you into leaving by pretending to be Baysinger and telling you about the time locks. But then you started that kidnapping business. I didn't want you to take me out of here because it meant leaving the suitcase; and if you did kidnap me, and I was forced to tell you the truth, you'd dump me somewhere and come back for the money yourselves. Now you've got it anyway—the game's up."

"That's for sure," One said.

I cleared my throat. "Tell you what," I said. "I'll split the eight thousand with you, half and half. That way, we all come out of this with something."

"I've got a better idea."

I knew what was coming, but I said, "What's that?"

"We take the whole boodle."

"Now wait a minute—"

"We've got the guns, and that means we make the rules. You're out of luck, Smith, or whatever your name is. You may have gotten here first, but we got here at the right time."

"Honor among thieves," I said. "Hah."

"Easy come, easy go," Two said. "You know how it is."

"All right, you're taking all the money. What about me?"

"What about you?"

"Do I get to walk out of here?"

"Well, we're sure as hell not going to call the cops on you."

"You did us sort of a favor," One said, "taking care of all the details before we got here. So we'll do you one. We'll tie you up in one of these chairs—not too tight, just tight enough to keep you here for ten or fifteen minutes. When you work yourself loose you're on your own."

"Why can't I just leave when you do?"

One gave me a faint smile. "Because you might get a bright idea to follow us and try to take the money back. We wouldn't like that."

I shook my head resignedly. "Some bank job this turned out to be."

They tied me up in the chair behind the desk, using my necktie and my belt to bind my hands and feet. After which they took the suitcase, and my Colt Woodsman, and went out through the rear door and left me alone.

It took me almost twenty minutes to work my hands loose. When they were free I leaned over to untie my feet and stood up wearily to work the kinks out of my arms and legs. Then I sat down again, pulled the phone over in front of me, and dialed a number.

A moment later a familiar voice said, "Police Chief Roberts speaking."

"This is Luther Baysinger, George," I said. "You'd better get over here to the bank right away. I've just been held up."

Chief Roberts was a tall wiry man in his early sixties, a competent law officer in his own ponderous way; I had known him for nearly thirty years. While his two underlings, Burt Young and Frank Dawes—the sum total of Fairfield's police force—hurried in and out, making radio calls and looking for fingerprints or clues or whatever, Roberts listened intently to my account of what had happened with the two bank robbers. When I finished he leaned back in the chair across the desk from me and wagged his head in an admiring way.

"Luther," he said, "you always did have more gall than any man in the county. But this business sure does take the cake for pure nerve."

"Am I to take that as a compliment, George?" I said a bit stiffly.

"Sure," he said. "Don't get your back up."

"The fact of the matter is, I had little choice. It was either pretend to be a bank robber myself or spend the weekend at the mercy of those two men. And have them steal all the money inside the vault on Monday morning—approximately forty thousand dollars, not twenty thousand as I told them."

"Lucky thing you had that Woodsman of yours along. That was probably the clincher."

"That, and the fact that I wasn't carrying my wallet. I was in such a hurry this morning that I left it on my dresser at home."

"How come you happened to have the .22?"

"It has been jamming on me in target practice lately," I said. "I intended to drop it off at Ben Ogilvie's gunsmith shop tonight for repairs."

"How'd you know those two hadn't cased the bank beforehand?"

"It was a simple deduction. If they had cased the bank, they would have known who I was; they wouldn't have had to ask."

Roberts wagged his head again. "You're something else, Luther. You really are."

"Mmm," I said. "Do you think you'll be able to apprehend them?"

"Oh, we'll get them, all right. The descriptions you gave us are pretty detailed; Burt's already sent them out to the county and state people and to the FBI."

"Fine." I massaged my temples. "I had better begin making an exact count of how much money they got away with. I've called the main branch in the capital and they're sending an official over as soon as possible. I imagine he'll be coming with the local FBI agent."

Roberts rose ponderously. "We'll leave you to it, then." He gathered Young and Dawes and prepared to leave. At the door he paused to grin at me. "Yes, sir," he said, "more damned gall—and more damned luck—than any man in this county."

I returned to my desk after they were gone and allowed myself a cigar. I felt vastly relieved. Fate, for once, had chosen to smile on me; I had, indeed, been lucky.

But for more reasons than Roberts thought.

I recalled his assurance that the bank robbers would soon be apprehended. Unfortunately—or fortunately, depending on the point of view—I did not believe they would be appre-hended at all. Mainly because the description of them I had given Roberts was totally inaccurate.

I had also altered my story in a number of other ways. I had told him the outer vault door had not only been un-locked—which was the truth; despite my lie to the two rob-bers, I had not set any of the time locks—but that it had been open and the money they'd stolen was from the cash room. I had said the robbers brought the suitcase with them, not that it belonged to me, and that the Woodsman had been in my overcoat pocket when they discovered it. I had omitted men-tion of the fact that I'd supposedly called their attention to the suitcase in order to carry out my bank-robber ruse.

And I had also lied about the reasons I was not carrying my wallet and why I had the Woodsman with me. In truth, I had left the wallet at home and put the gun into the suitcase be-cause of an impulsive, foolish, and half-formed idea that, later tonight, I would attempt to hold up a business establish-ment or two somewhere in the next county.

I would almost certainly *not* have gone through with that scheme, but the point was that I had got myself into a rather desperate situation. The bank examiners were due on Monday for their annual audit—a month earlier than usual in a surprise announcement—and I had not been able to replace all of the $14,425.00 that I had "borrowed" during the past ten months to support my regrettable penchant for betting on losing horses.

I had, however, managed on short notice to raise $8,370.00 by selling my car and my small boat and disposing of certain semi-valuable heirlooms. The very same $8,370.00 that had been in the suitcase, and that I had been about to *put back* into the cash room when the two robbers arrived.

As things had turned out, I no longer had to worry about

replacing the money or about the bank examiners discovering my peccadillo. Of course, I would have to be considerably more prudent in the future where my predilection for the Sport of Kings was concerned. And I would be; I am not one to make the same mistake twice. I may have a lot of gall, as Roberts had phrased it, and I may be something of a rogue, but for all that I'm neither a bad nor an unwise fellow. After all, I *had* saved most of the bank's money, hadn't I?

I relaxed with my cigar. Because I had done my "borrowing" from the vault assets without falsifying bank records, I had nothing to do now except to wait patiently for the official and the FBI agent to arrive from the state capital. And when they did, I would tell them the literal truth.

"The exact total of the theft," I would say, "is $14,425.00."

And Then We Went To Venus

Three weeks after the return of Commander Richard Stiles and Major Philip Webber—the two-man crew of Exploration V, the first manned "supership" to land on Venus—and the sudden, unexplained, and total information blackout by both NASA and Washington, a security leak from "an unimpeachable source" blew the lid off the whole thing. If it had not been for that, the news media and the general population might not have gotten the details on the mission for months or years, if they had gotten them at all.

Until the leak, all any of us knew was that Exploration V had made the Venus landing and in it Stiles and Webber had spent some twelve undocumented hours on the surface of the planet (the ship's entire communication system had malfunctioned shortly after lift-off); that Mission Control had effected Venus lift-off and return; and that re-entry touchdown had been little more than routine. Full news media coverage was encouraged up to that point, of course. We had landed on the moon and we had landed on Mars, and now that government metallurgists had developed a breakthrough alloy able to withstand temperatures in excess of one thousand degrees Fahrenheit, we had landed on Venus—yet another great moment in the history of Mankind. But the official lid dropped and sealed as soon as NASA personnel opened up the capsule. The only other fact we knew for certain was that astronauts Stiles and Webber were alive.

During those three weeks a breathless expectation, and an air of apprehension, gripped the world at large. Why the secrecy, why the silence? I asked those questions myself, in print in my syndicated political column, and feared the answers perhaps more than most. I had long been a professional skeptic, about any number of things including certain "blind-leap" aspects of our re-augmented space program. It seemed to me we did too many things on the basis of insufficient data; our thirst for knowledge sometimes took precedence over other considerations, not the least of which was human safety. NASA was as much an offender in this respect as any other government agency.

The *Washington Post* broke the story, in a rare banner headline. Within hours it was on every front page of every newspaper in every nation, and on every television and radio station, and on every tongue.

There were two major revelations.

First, both Commander Stiles and Major Webber had returned from the mission suffering from what was termed "severe mental disability."

And, second, NASA was said to possess a certain amount of evidence that a form of sentient life existed on the planet Venus.

It was, of course, the latter which initiated the most reaction and to which the most lip service was paid. Life on Venus, sentient life on another planet in our solar system; fiction and endless speculation apparently proved fact. It was a startling, exciting, somewhat frightening possibility. What did the life look like? Was it intelligent? If so, could we establish contact? Would it be friendly or unfriendly? What kind of culture could it have on that wet, steaming, vapor-obscured planet? And on and on.

But one of the key questions, as far as I was concerned, was: What had happened to Stiles and Webber?

Economic, civil, political, and personal crises were forgotten; everyone wanted to Know More. NASA and Washington at first attempted to discredit the *Post* report; but, as with the Pentagon Papers and Watergate decades earlier, the facts discredited the attempt to discredit the facts. The public hue and cry was overwhelming, so much so that it could not be ignored. Ultimately there was nothing NASA and Washington could do, especially in view of the fact that this was an election year, except to yield with a stiff grace.

The President called a closed-door press conference in the White House press room, and my credentials got me a front-row seat. He appeared first and made a few introductory remarks about "the grave importance of the knowledge which may await us in limitless space." After which, wisely, he turned the conference over to uniformed and beribboned General Joseph Meadows, one of the top men in NASA and the head of the Venus Exploration program.

To begin with, Meadows distributed copies of a prepared press release which corroborated, in typical vague governmental fashion, the two main facts reported in the *Post*. The general read the release aloud; then, with some apparent reluctance, he called for questions.

"What are the physical characteristics of the life on Venus, General?"

"I am unable to answer that question. We simply do not know."

"It *is* sentient, however, is that correct?"

"We believe that it may be."

"Could it be intelligent?"

"We don't know and cannot speculate."

"Just what leads you to believe that a life form exists on Venus?"

"We have certain photographic evidence, recorded by the automatic cameras on Exploration Five, which bears out that supposition."

"What sort of photographic evidence?"

"The film in question depicts a certain blurred activity on the portion of the planet's day-side land surface where the ship touched down."

"Cities, do you mean? A culture of some kind?"

"No. Activity, movement—simply that."

"Can't you be more specific?"

"I'm sorry, I cannot."

"Was similar photographic evidence transmitted by the cameras in the unmanned Exploration Three and Exploration Four capsules?"

"It was not."

"How do you account for that, sir?"

"I can only say that the Exploration Five landing took place at a markedly different spot on Venus than did either of the other two landings. Previous photographs, plus radar maps of the planet's surface and other recorded data, prepared us to believe that there were no life forms of any kind."

"What can you tell us about the surface of Venus, other than what we already know?"

"At this time, nothing at all."

"Is another Exploration mission being planned for the near future?"

"An announcement as to future plans will be made shortly."

"Assuming the life form is intelligent, will efforts be made to establish contact?"

"Certainly. But we have no current basis for such an assumption. We are proceeding one step at a time."

"About Commander Stiles and Major Webber, sir," I said. "What can you tell us about the nature of their illnesses?"

"Not a great deal, I'm afraid. Exhaustive tests are still being undertaken."

"Both men *are* alive?"

"Yes."

"What form of mental disorder is each suffering from?"

Pause. "Major Webber's condition may be loosely described as catatonic; Commander Stiles' condition as semi-catatonic."

"Does that mean you've been able to communicate with the commander?"

"No, it does not."

"Well, has he been lucid at any time?"

"I am not at liberty to answer that question."

"Have you been able to learn anything from him about what happened on Venus?"

"I am not at liberty to answer that."

"General, what do you suppose is responsible for these similar psychological disorders in Stiles and Webber? Based on available information, that is."

"All available information is still being tabulated; at present we have been able to draw no definite conclusions. However, it is possible that spatial stresses may be a primary factor."

"Isn't it rather improbable, sir, that two well-trained men would succumb to spatial stresses in the same way at approximately the same time?"

"The existence of sentient life on Venus is rather improbable. And yet it may one day prove to be fact."

"What about other possible explanations?" someone else asked. "Could these mental disorders have been caused by something of a physical nature? The 900-degree surface temperature, for example?"

"Negative. The Exploration Five capsule was not heat-damaged in any way; Commander Stiles and Major Webber did not leave the ship and could not have been affected by outside temperatures while inside it. And were not, as tests have proven."

"Magnetic fields or solar winds, then? The planet's atmosphere is composed of carbon dioxide and sulfuric acid, after all. . . ."

"Also negative. Harmful atmospheric elements could not have penetrated or affected conditions inside the capsule."

"Do you have any idea *when* either man was stricken?"

"We do not."

"Could it have happened prior to landing on Venus?"

"That is unlikely. Despite the malfunction of the communications system, both men performed other duties according to schedule."

"But they did not perform any duties after Mission Control effected lift-off from Venus for the return flight?"

"Correct."

"Then the mental disabilities occurred during the twelve hours Exploration Five was on the planet itself."

"It would appear so, yes."

I asked, "Have you considered the possibility, sir, that the alleged Venus life form was in some way responsible for the breakdowns of the two men?"

"We have, just as we have considered every other possibility. And we find it negative as well. There is no way a life form of any kind, not even a microscopic organism, could have penetrated the seal on the capsule. Exploration Five's instruments are highly sophisticated; they would have recorded—and we would subsequently have found—any evidence of such a penetration."

"Can you tell us, please, where Commander Stiles and Major Webber are now undergoing treatment?"

"I'm afraid not. That is classified information."

"Would it be possible for members of the media to see either or both of them?"

"At this time it would not."

It was anything but an enlightening session. We took what little Meadows had given us and passed it along to the hungry populace, but no one was satisfied. A little knowledge can be more provocative than no knowledge at all, as NASA's scientists knew better than anyone; in a situation of this magnitude, it only served to escalate matters into a fever pitch.

More pressure was applied from groups and factions and individuals. Politicians up for re-election, particularly those from the party out of power, seized the opportunity to make "the Venus life question" a major political issue. There was a kind of mass hysteria involved in all of this—a quivering excitement, a delicious fear. The silent cry from all sides seemed to be: "Tell us the worst, if that's what it is. Scare hell out of us, we can take it. Just don't keep us in the dark."

The furor brought results, after a fashion. NASA and Washington steadfastly refused to release any further details, or to embellish on those few which General Meadows had given out. They maintained the position that when they had facts, not suppositions, they would release them to the public. But again, because of the political pressure and because it *was* an election year, they had to make some kind of concession. And so they made one.

They agreed to allow a representative cross-section of the media to have a look at, although not to photograph, Commander Richard Stiles and Major Philip Webber.

I was among the seven men and three women chosen for the visit to the Virginia-based, government-maintained medical facility in which the astronauts were undergoing "interim treatment." The selection was supposedly made at random, but, in truth, it was only those of us with upper echelon clout who were invited. I had to call in two favors and make half a dozen promises, and even then I wasn't sure I was going to be included until the day before the visit was scheduled.

It was on a morning exactly five weeks after the return of Exploration V that NASA personnel, operating under tight security measures, escorted the ten of us to the medical facility. Once inside, we were met by Doctor Benjamin Fuller, a government psychologist and Ph.D. who specialized in mental disorders and who was in charge of the care and treatment of Stiles and Webber. He allowed us a brief question-and-answer period, but his responses were just as noncommittal as General Meadows' had been earlier.

No, he was not prepared to say whether or not either astronaut was responding to treatment, or if any information had been gleaned from them on the Venus landing.

No, he had no opinion at this time as to whether or not a complete or partial cure could be gained in either case.

No, he was not at liberty to divulge the nature of the treatments being used on the two men.

Yes, the official view as to the cause of their disability was still the same: undefined spatial stresses.

Doctor Fuller then conducted us through a maze of sterile hallways, peopled with sterile, plastic-featured medical types. At length we came to a large room which had a kind of drapery drawn across one wall. Fuller asked that we maintain silence and that we line up to file past one at a time; then he went to the wall and opened the drapery.

Behind it was a window—or, rather, a two-way glass which was a window from our side. Through the glass, when my turn came, I saw an oblong white room containing a bed and two tubular chairs and a tubular nightstand. On the bed, motionless, lay Major Philip Webber.

If I had not known he was thirty-six years old, I would have thought he was a man in his sixties. His hair had turned almost white and the skin of his face was loose, wattled; his eyes were blank and fixed, sunken deep in their sockets. He might have been dead except for the rhythmic rise and fall of his chest.

I felt my stomach constrict as I looked at him. A man in superb physical condition, who had undergone rigorous training and test conditioning in preparation for the Exploration V mission. A shell, a vegetable.

As soon as the last of us had had his turn at the glass, Fuller reclosed the drapery and gestured us out into the corridor again. None of us spoke; there was nothing to say. We followed him to another room similar to the first. Here, now, we would see Commander Richard Stiles—the most qualified man in America to captain Man's first landing on Venus, an accomplished logician, a technological genius.

We queued up near the wall and Fuller opened the cloth.

I was last in line this time; but from the faces of the others as they turned away I could tell that, if anything, Stiles was in worse shape than Webber. And he was. When I finally stepped up to the glass, I saw him sitting on a white chair, in profile at the foot of his bed. His hands were clasped so tightly together in his lap that the straining tendons in both wrists were visible. Only his lips moved, as if he were muttering to himself. Like Webber, his eyes stared at nothing—and like Webber, he looked at least twenty years older than his age of forty-one.

My stomach knotted again. I wanted suddenly to get out of that room, out of that building and into the sunlight. I started to turn aside.

Stiles moved.

He came to his feet with startling abruptness, spun out of profile, and took four long steps toward the glass. From his side it was only a mirror returning his own image to him, and yet it was as if he had sensed that someone was there, watching him. A glimmer of intelligence seemed to come into his eyes.

And his mouth opened and framed a word.

If he spoke that word aloud, I couldn't hear it; the room was probably soundproofed. But I saw clearly the movement of his lips, and I understood—was sure I understood—what the word was. It brought chills to my back, made me take an involuntary step backward.

Grim-faced, Doctor Fuller brushed past me and pulled the drapery shut. When I caught his eye, he met my gaze with an expression that revealed nothing. I looked at the others then, but none of them had understood what Stiles had said; I would have seen it in their faces if they had.

"Ladies and gentlemen," Fuller said in the corridor outside, "I must ask you to confine your reports of what you've witnessed here today to factual impressions. Irresponsible speculation of any kind, particularly that based on uncertain visual interpretation, will not be tolerated." He was looking straight at me as he said it.

Once we had been returned to our point of departure in downtown Washington, I left the others, and went to the nearest bar and drank two double bourbons. I was shaken, badly shaken. Fuller had made it clear that there would be severe repercussions if I printed what I thought I'd heard Stiles say; but his warning was unnecessary. I had no intention of printing it.

The public had a right to know, yes; they were desperate to know. *Scare hell out of us, we can take it.* But could they? I wasn't so sure. The implications in that single word were enough to sow the seeds of panic. . . .

I was about to order a third drink when Joe Anders came into the place. He was another newsman, a UPI correspondent whom I knew on a first name basis. He sat down next to me and called for a draft beer.

"Little early in the day for you, isn't it?" he asked.

"Not today it isn't."

"That bad, huh?"

"What?"

"Seeing Stiles and Webber."

"Yes," I said. "Very bad."

"Want to talk about it?"

"No."

"Suit yourself," he said, and shrugged. "Latest poop on the Venus situation is bigger news, anyway."

I sat up straight. "What latest poop?"

"You mean you haven't heard?"

"I haven't checked in with my office. What is it?"

"Well, it's not official yet, but NASA's expected to make the announcement within a week. Plans are under way for Exploration Six, to confirm or deny the Venus life question. Six-man crew this time, including a biologist and a linguist. Just in case."

"Oh my God," I said.

Anders said something else, but I didn't hear it. Six more men, I was thinking. Six more just like Stiles and Webber? And how many after that? How many others before they accepted the truth?

If it *was* the truth.

NASA didn't think it was; they knew what I knew, of course, but the possibility was beyond their collective scientific minds. Maybe they were right. I prayed to God they were.

But the image of Stiles' face was sharp and terrible in my mind, and so was that word I believed I had seen him speak. The one word that told nothing and yet may have told everything about what had happened to him and Webber, about what awaited all men who landed on Venus.

The word "Medusa."

Putting the Pieces Back

You wouldn't think a man could change completely in four months—but when Kaprelian saw Fred DeBeque come walking into the Drop Back Inn, he had living proof that it could happen. He was so startled, in fact, that he just stood there behind the plank and stared with his mouth hanging open.

It had been a rainy off-Monday exactly like this one the last time he'd seen DeBeque, and that night the guy had been about as low as you could get and carrying a load big enough for two. Now he was dressed in a nice tailored suit, looking sober and normal as though he'd never been through any heavy personal tragedy. Kaprelian felt this funny sense of flashback come over him, like the entire last seven months hadn't even existed.

He didn't much care for feelings like that, and he shook it off. Then he smiled kind of sadly as DeBeque walked over and took his old stool, the one he'd sat on every night for the three months after he had come home from work late one afternoon and found his wife bludgeoned to death.

Actually, Kaprelian was glad to see the change in him. He hadn't known DeBeque or DeBeque's wife very well before the murder; they were just people who lived in the neighborhood and dropped in once in a while for a drink. He'd liked them both though, and he'd gotten to know Fred pretty well afterward, while he was doing that boozing. That was why the change surprised him as much as it did. He'd been sure DeBeque would turn into a Skid Row bum or a corpse, the way he put down the sauce; a man couldn't drink like that more than maybe a year without ending up one or the other.

The thing was, DeBeque and his wife really loved each other. He'd been crazy for her, worshipped the ground she walked on—Kaprelian had never loved anybody that way, so he couldn't really understand it. Anyhow, when she'd been murdered DeBeque had gone all to pieces. Without her, he'd told Kaprelian a few times, he didn't want to go on living himself; but he didn't have the courage to kill himself either. Except with the bottle.

There was another reason why he couldn't kill himself, DeBeque said, and that was because he wanted to see the murderer punished and the police hadn't yet caught him. They'd sniffed around DeBeque himself at first, but he had an alibi and, anyway, all his and her friends told them how much the two of them were in love. So then, even though nobody had seen any suspicious types in the neighborhood the day it happened, the cops had worked around with the theory that it was either a junkie who'd forced his way into the DeBeque apartment or a sneak thief that she'd surprised. The place had been ransacked and there was some jewelry and mad money missing. Her skull had been crushed with a lamp, and the cops figured she had tried to put up a fight.

So DeBeque kept coming to the Drop Back Inn every night and getting drunk and waiting for the cops to find his wife's killer. After three months went by, they still hadn't found the guy. The way it looked to Kaprelian then—and so far that was the way it had turned out—they never would. The last night he'd seen DeBeque, Fred had admitted that same thing for the first time and then he had walked out into the rain and vanished. Until just now.

Kaprelian said, "Fred, it's good to see you. I been wondering what happened to you, you disappeared so sudden four months ago."

"I guess you never expected I'd show up again, did you, Harry?"

"You want the truth, I sure didn't. But you really look great. Where you been all this time?"

"Putting the pieces back together again," DeBeque said. "Finding new meaning in life."

Kaprelian nodded. "You know, I thought you were headed for Skid Row or an early grave, you don't mind my saying so."

"No, I don't mind. You're absolutely right, Harry."

"Well—can I get you a drink?"

"Ginger ale," DeBeque said. "I'm off alcohol now."

Kaprelian was even more surprised. There are some guys, some drinkers, you don't ever figure *can* quit, and that was how DeBeque had struck him at the tag end of those three bad months. He said, "Me being a bar owner, I shouldn't say this, but I'm glad to hear that too. If there's one thing I learned after twenty years in this business, you can't drown your troubles or your sorrows in the juice. I seen hundreds try and not one succeed."

"You tried to tell me that a dozen times, as I recall," DeBeque said. "Fortunately, I realized you were right in time to do something about it."

Kaprelian scooped ice into a glass and filled it with ginger ale from the automatic hand dispenser. When he set the glass on the bar, one of the two workers down at the other end—the only other customers in the place—called to him for another beer. He drew it and took it down and then came back to lean on the bar in front of DeBeque.

"So where'd you go after you left four months ago?" he asked. "I mean, did you stay here in the city or what? I know you moved out of the neighborhood."

"No, I didn't stay here." DeBeque sipped his ginger ale.

"It's funny the way insights come to a man, Harry—and funny how long it takes sometimes. I spent three months not caring about anything, drinking myself to death, drowning in self-pity; then one morning I just woke up knowing I couldn't go on that way any longer. I wasn't sure why, but I knew I had to straighten myself out. I went upstate and dried out in a rented cabin in the mountains. The rest of the insight came there: I knew why I'd stopped drinking, what it was I had to do."

"What was that, Fred?"

"Find the man who murdered Karen."

Kaprelian had been listening with rapt attention. What DeBeque had turned into wasn't a bum or a corpse but the kind of comeback hero you see in television crime dramas and don't believe for a minute. When you heard it like this, though, in real life and straight from the gut, you knew it had to be the truth—and it made you feel good.

Still, it wasn't the most sensible decision DeBeque could have reached, not in real life, and Kaprelian said, "I don't know, Fred, if the cops couldn't find the guy—"

DeBeque nodded. "I went through all the objections myself," he said, "but I knew I still had to try. So I came back here to the city and I started looking. I spent a lot of time in the Tenderloin bars, and I got to know a few street people, got in with them, was more or less accepted by them. After a while I started asking questions and getting answers."

"You mean," Kaprelian said, astonished, "you actually got a line on the guy who did it?"

Smiling, DeBeque said, "No. All the answers I got were negative. No, Harry, I learned absolutely nothing—except that the police were wrong about the man who killed Karen. He wasn't a junkie or a sneak thief or a street criminal of any kind."

"Then who was he?"

"Someone who knew her, someone she trusted. Someone she would let in the apartment."

"Makes sense, I guess," Kaprelian said. "You have any idea who this someone could be?"

"Not at first. But after I did some discreet investigating, after I visited the neighborhood again a few times, it all came together like the answer to a mathematical equation. There was only one person it could be."

"Who?" Kaprelian asked.

"The mailman."

"The *mailman?*"

"Of course. Think about it, Harry. Who else would have easy access to our apartment? Who else could even be seen entering the apartment by neighbors without them thinking anything of it, or even remembering it later? The mailman."

"Well, what did you do?"

"I found out his name and I went to see him one night last week. I confronted him with knowledge of his guilt. He denied it, naturally; he kept right on denying it to the end."

"The end?"

"When I killed him," DeBeque said.

Kaprelian's neck went cold. "Killed him? Fred, you can't be serious! You didn't actually *kill* him—"

"Don't sound so shocked," DeBeque said. "What else could I do? I had no evidence, I couldn't take him to the police. But neither could I allow him to get away with what he'd done to Karen. You understand that, don't you? I had no choice. I took out the gun I'd picked up in a pawnshop, and I shot him with it—right through the heart."

"Jeez," Kaprelian said. "Jeez."

DeBeque stopped smiling then and frowned down into his ginger ale; he was silent, kind of moody all of a sudden.

Kaprelian became aware of how quiet it was and flipped on the TV. While he was doing that the two workers got up from their stools at the other end of the bar, waved at him, and went on out.

DeBeque said suddenly, "Only then I realized he couldn't have been the one."

Kaprelian turned from the TV. "What?"

"It couldn't have been the mailman," DeBeque said. "He was left-handed, and the police established that the killer was probably right-handed. Something about the angle of the blow that killed Karen. So I started thinking who else it could have been, and then I knew: the grocery delivery boy. Except we used two groceries, two delivery boys, and it turned out both of them were right-handed. I talked to the first and I was sure he was the one. I shot him. Then I knew I'd been wrong, it was the other one. I shot him too."

"Hey," Kaprelian said. "Hey, Fred, what're you *saying?*"

"But it wasn't the delivery boys either." DeBeque's eyes were very bright. "Who, then? Somebody else from the neighborhood . . . and it came to me, I knew who it had to be."

Kaprelian still didn't quite grasp what he was hearing. It was all coming too fast. "Who?" he said.

"You," DeBeque said, and it wasn't until he pulled the gun that Kaprelian finally understood what was happening, what DeBeque had *really* turned into after those three grieving, alcoholic months. Only by then it was too late.

The last thing he heard was voices on the television—a crime drama, one of those where the guy's wife is murdered and he goes out and finds the real killer and ends up a hero in time for the last commercial. . . .

The Arrowmont Prison Riddle

I first met the man who called himself by the unlikely name of Buckmaster Gilloon in the late summer of 1916, my second year as warden of Arrowmont Prison. There were no living quarters within the old brick walls of the prison, which was situated on a promontory overlooking a small winding river two miles north of Arrowmont Village, so I had rented a cottage in the village proper, not far from a tavern known as Hallahan's Irish Inn. It was in this tavern, and as a result of a mutual passion for Guinness stout and the game of darts, that Gilloon and I became acquainted.

As a man he was every bit as unlikely as his name. He was in his late thirties, short and almost painfully thin; he had a glass eye and a drooping and incongruous Oriental-style mustache, wore English tweeds, gaudy Albert watch chains and plaid Scotch caps, and always carried half a dozen loose-leaf notebooks in which he perpetually and secretively jotted things. He was well read and erudite, had a repertoire of bawdy stories to rival any vaudevillian in the country, and never seemed to lack ready cash. He lived in a boarding house in the center of the village and claimed to be a writer for the pulp magazines—*Argosy*, *Adventure*, *All-Story Weekly*, *Munsey*'s. Perhaps he was, but he steadfastly refused to discuss any of his fiction, or to divulge his pseudonym or pseudonyms.

He was reticent about divulging any personal information. When personal questions arose, he deftly changed the subject. Since he did not speak with an accent, I took him to be American-born. I was able to learn, from occasional comments and observations, that he had traveled extensively throughout the world.

In my nine decades on this earth I have never encountered a more fascinating or troubling enigma than this man whose path crossed mine for a few short weeks in 1916.

Who and what was Buckmaster Gilloon? Is it possible for one enigma to be attracted and motivated by another enigma? Can that which seems natural and coincidental be the result instead of preternatural forces? These questions have plagued me in the sixty years since Gilloon and I became involved in what appeared to be an utterly enigmatic crime.

It all began on September 26, 1916—the day of the scheduled execution at Arrowmont Prison of a condemned murderer named Arthur Teasdale . . .

Shortly before noon of that day a thunderstorm struck without warning. Rain pelted down from a black sky, and lightning crackled in low jagged blazes that gave the illusion of striking unseen objects just beyond the prison walls. I was already suffering from nervous tension, as was always the case on the day of an execution, and the storm added to my discomfort. I passed the early afternoon sitting at my desk, staring out the window, listening to the inexorable ticking of my Seth Thomas, wishing the execution was done with and it was eight o'clock, when I was due to meet Gilloon at Hallahan's for Guinness and darts.

At 3:30 the two civilians who had volunteered to act as witnesses to the hanging arrived. I ushered them into a waiting room and asked them to wait until they were summoned. Then I donned a slicker and stopped by the office of Rogers, the chief guard, and asked him to accompany me to the execution shed.

The shed was relatively small, constructed of brick with a

tin roof, and sat in a corner of the prison between the textile mill and the iron foundry. It was lighted by lanterns hung from the walls and the rafters and contained only a row of witness chairs and a high permanent gallows at the far end. Attached to the shed's north wall was an annex in which the death cell was located. As was customary, Teasdale had been transported there five days earlier to await due process.

He was a particularly vicious and evil man, Teasdale. He had cold-bloodedly murdered three people during an abortive robbery attempt in the state capital, and had been anything but a model prisoner during his month's confinement at Arrowmont. As a rule I had a certain compassion for those condemned to hang under my jurisdiction, and in two cases I had spoken to the governor in favor of clemency. In Teasdale's case, however, I had conceded that a continuance of his life would serve no good purpose.

When I had visited him the previous night to ask if he wished to see a clergyman or to order anything special for his last meal, he had cursed me and Rogers and the entire prison personnel with an almost maniacal intensity, vowing vengeance on us all from the grave.

I rather expected, as Rogers and I entered the death cell at ten minutes of four, to find Teasdale in much the same state. However, he had fallen instead into an acute melancholia; he lay on his cot with his knees drawn up and his eyes staring blankly at the opposite wall. The two guards assigned to him, Hollowell and Granger (Granger was also the state-appointed hangman), told us he had been like that for several hours. I spoke to him, asking again if he wished to confer with a clergyman. He did not answer, did not move. I inquired if he had any last requests, and if it was his wish to wear a hood for his final walk to the gallows and for the execution. He did not respond.

I took Hollowell aside. "Perhaps it would be better to use the hood," I said. "It will make it easier for all of us."

"Yes, sir."

Rogers and I left the annex, accompanied by Granger, for a final examination of the gallows. The rope had already been hung and the hangman's knot tied. While Granger made certain they were secure I unlocked the door beneath the platform, which opened into a short passage that ended in a narrow cubicle beneath the trap. The platform had been built eight feet off the floor, so that the death throes of the condemned man would be concealed from the witnesses—a humane gesture which was not observed by all prisons in our state, and for which I was grateful.

After I had made a routine examination of the cubicle, and re-locked the door, I mounted the thirteen steps to the platform. The trap beneath the gibbet arm was operated by a lever set into the floor; when Granger threw the lever, the trap would fall open. Once we tried it and reset it, I pronounced everything in readiness and sent Rogers to summon the civilian witnesses and the prison doctor. It was then 4:35 and the execution would take place at precisely five o'clock. I had received a wire from the governor the night before, informing me that there wasn't the remotest chance of a stay being granted.

When Rogers returned with the witnesses and the doctor, we all took chairs in the row arranged some forty feet opposite the gallows. Time passed, tensely; with thunder echoing outside, a hard rain drumming against the tin roof, and eerie shadows not entirely dispelled by the lanternlight, the moments before that execution were particularly disquieting.

I held my pocket watch open on my knee, and at 4:55 I signaled to the guard at the annex door to call for the prisoner. Three more minutes crept by and then the door reopened and

Granger and Hollowell brought Teasdale into the shed.

The three men made a grim procession as they crossed to the gallows steps: Granger in his black hangman's duster, Hollowell in his khaki guard uniform and peaked cap, Teasdale between them in his grey prison clothing and black hood. Teasdale's shoes dragged across the floor—he was a stiffly unresisting weight until they reached the steps; then he struggled briefly and Granger and Hollowell were forced to tighten their grip and all but carry him up onto the gallows. Hollowell held him slumped on the trap while Granger solemnly fitted the noose around his neck and drew it taut.

The hands on my watch read five o'clock when, as prescribed by law, Granger intoned, "Have you any last words before the sentence imposed on you is carried out?"

Teasdale said nothing, but his body twisted with a spasm of fear.

Granger looked in my direction and I raised my hand to indicate final sanction. He backed away from Teasdale and rested his hand on the release lever. As he did so, there came from outside a long, rolling peal of thunder that seemed to shake the shed roof. A chill touched the nape of my neck and I shifted uneasily on my chair.

Just as the sound of the thunder faded, Granger threw the lever and Hollowell released Teasdale and stepped back. The trap thudded open and the condemned man plummeted downward.

In that same instant I thought I saw a faint silvery glimmer above the opening, but it was so brief that I took it for an optical illusion. My attention was focused on the rope: it danced for a moment under the weight of the body, then pulled taut and became motionless. I let out a soft tired sigh and sat forward while Granger and Hollowell, both of whom were looking away from the open trap, silently counted off the passage of sixty seconds.

When the minute had elapsed, Granger turned and walked to the edge of the trap. If the body hung laxly, he would signal to me so that the prison doctor and I could enter the cubicle and officially pronounce Teasdale deceased; if the body was still thrashing, thus indicating the condemned man's neck had not been broken in the fall—grisly prospect, but I had seen it happen—more time would be allowed to pass. It sounds brutal, I know, but such was the law and it had to be obeyed without question.

But Granger's reaction was so peculiar and so violent that I came immediately to my feet. He flinched as if he had been struck in the stomach and his face twisted into an expression of disbelief. He dropped to his hands and knees at the front of the trap as Hollowell came up beside him and leaned down to peer into the passageway.

"What is it, Granger?" I called. "What's the matter?"

He straightened after a few seconds and pivoted toward me. "You better get up here, Warden Parker," he said. His voice was shrill and tremulous and he clutched at his stomach. "Quick!"

Rogers and I exchanged glances, then ran to the steps, mounted them, and hurried to the trap, the other guards and the prison doctor close behind us. As soon as I looked downward, it was my turn to stare with incredulity, to exclaim against what I saw—and what I did not see.

The hangman's noose at the end of the rope was empty.

Except for the black hood on the ground, the cubicle was empty.

Impossibly, the body of Arthur Teasdale had vanished.

I raced down the gallows steps and fumbled the platform

door open with my key. I had the vague desperate hope that Teasdale had somehow slipped the noose and that I would see him lying within, against the door—that small section of the passageway was shrouded in darkness and not quite penetrable from above—but he wasn't there. The passageway, like the cubicle, was deserted.

While I called for a lantern Rogers hoisted up the rope to examine it and the noose. A moment later he announced that it had not been tampered with in any way. When a guard brought the lantern I embarked on a careful search of the area, but there were no loose boards in the walls of the passage or the cubicle, and the floor was of solid concrete. On the floor I discovered a thin sliver of wood about an inch long, which may or may not have been there previously. Aside from that, there was not so much as a strand of hair or a loose thread to be found. And the black hood told me nothing at all.

There simply did not seem to be any way Teasdale—or his remains—could have gotten, or been gotten, out of there.

I stood for a moment, staring at the flickering light from the lantern, listening to the distant rumbling of thunder. *Had* Teasdale died at the end of the hangman's rope? Or had he somehow managed to cheat death? I had seen him fall through the trap with my own eyes, had seen the rope dance and then pull taut with the weight of his body. He *must* have expired, I told myself.

A shiver moved along my back. I found myself remembering Teasdale's threats to wreak vengeance from the grave, and I had the irrational thought that perhaps something otherworldly had been responsible for the phenomenon we had witnessed. Teasdale had, after all, been a malignant individual. Could he have been so evil that he had managed to summon the Powers of Darkness to save him in the instant before death—or to claim him soul *and* body in the instant after it?

I refused to believe it. I am a practical man, not prone to superstition, and it has always been my nature to seek a logical explanation for even the most uncommon occurrence. Arthur Teasdale had disappeared, yes; but it could not be other than an earthly force behind the deed. Which meant that, alive or dead, Teasdale was still somewhere inside the walls of Arrowmont Prison.

I roused myself, left the passageway, and issued instructions for a thorough search of the prison grounds. I ordered word sent to the guards in the watchtowers to double their normal vigilance. I noticed that Hollowell wasn't present along with the assembled guards and asked where he had gone. One of the others said he had seen Hollowell hurry out of the shed several minutes earlier.

Frowning, I pondered this information. Had Hollowell intuited something, or even seen something, and gone off unwisely to investigate on his own rather than confide in the rest of us? He had been employed at Arrowmont Prison less than two months, so I knew relatively little about him. I requested that he be found and brought to my office.

When Rogers and Granger and the other guards had departed, I escorted the two civilian witnesses to the administration building, where I asked them to remain until the mystery was explained. As I settled grimly at my desk to await Hollowell and word on the search of the grounds, I expected such an explanation within the hour.

I could not, however, have been more wrong.

The first development came after thirty minutes, and it was nearly as alarming as the disappearance of Teasdale from the gallows cubicle. One of the guards brought the news that a body had been discovered behind a stack of lumber in a lean-to between the execution shed and the iron foundry. But it was not the body of Arthur Teasdale.

It was that of Hollowell, stabbed to death with an awl.

I went immediately. As I stood beneath the rain-swept lean-to, looking down at the bloody front of poor Hollowell's uniform, a fresh set of unsettling questions tumbled through my mind. Had he been killed because, as I had first thought, he had either seen or intuited something connected with Teasdale's disappearance? If that was the case, whatever it was had died with him.

Or was it possible that he had himself been involved in the disappearance and been murdered to assure his silence? But how could he have been involved? He had been in my sight the entire time on the gallows platform. He had done nothing suspicious, could not in any way I could conceive have assisted in the deed.

How could Teasdale have survived the hanging?

How could he have escaped not only the gallows but the execution shed itself?

The only explanation seemed to be that it was not a live Arthur Teasdale who was carrying out his warped revenge, but a dead one who had been embraced and given earthly powers by the Forces of Evil . . .

In order to dispel the dark reflections from my mind, I personally supervised the balance of the search. Tines of lightning split the sky and thunder continued to hammer the roofs as we went from building to building. No corner of the prison compound escaped our scrutiny. No potential hiding place was overlooked. We went so far as to test for the presence of tunnels in the work areas and in the individual cells, although I had instructed just such a search only weeks before as part of my security program.

We found nothing.

Alive or dead, Arthur Teasdale was no longer within the walls of Arrowmont Prison.

I left the prison at ten o'clock that night. There was nothing more to be done, and I was filled with such depression and anxiety that I could not bear to spend another minute there. I had debated contacting the governor, of course, and, wisely or not, had decided against it for the time being. He would think me a lunatic if I requested assistance in a county or statewide search for a man who had for all intents and purposes been hanged at five o'clock that afternoon. If there were no new developments within the next twenty-four hours, I knew I would have no choice but to explain the situation to him. And I had no doubt that such an explanation unaccompanied by Teasdale or Teasdale's remains would cost me my position.

Before leaving, I swore everyone to secrecy, saying that I would have any man's job if he leaked word of the day's events to the press or to the public-at-large. The last thing I wanted was rumor-mongering and a general panic as a result of it. I warned Granger and the other guards who had come in contact with Teasdale to be especially wary and left word that I was to be contacted immediately if there were any further developments before morning.

I had up to that time given little thought to my own safety. But when I reached my cottage in the village I found myself imagining menace in every shadow and sound. Relaxation was impossible. After twenty minutes I felt impelled to leave, to seek out a friendly face. I told my housekeeper I would be at Hallahan's Irish Inn if anyone called for me and drove my Packard to the tavern.

The first person I saw upon entering was Buckmaster Gilloon. He was seated alone in a corner booth, writing in one of his notebooks, a stein of draught Guinness at his elbow.

Gilloon had always been very secretive about his note-books and never allowed anyone to glimpse so much as a word of what he put into them. But he was so engrossed when I walked up to the booth that he did not hear me, and I happened to glance down at the open page on which he was writing. There was but a single interrogative sentence on the page, clearly legible in his bold hand. The sentence read:

If a jimbuck stands alone by the sea, on a night when the dark moon sings, how many grains of sand in a single one of his foot-prints?

That sentence has always haunted me, because I cannot begin to understand its significance. I have no idea what a jimbuck is, except perhaps as a fictional creation, and yet that passage was like none which ever appeared in such periodicals as *Argosy* or *Munsey*'s.

Gilloon sensed my presence after a second or two, and he slammed the notebook slut. A ferocious scowl crossed his normally placid features. He said irritably, "Reading over a man's shoulder is a nasty habit, Parker."

"I'm sorry, I didn't mean to pry—"

"I'll thank you to be more respectful of my privacy in the future."

"Yes, of course." I sank wearily into the booth opposite him and called for a Guinness.

Gilloon studied me across the table. "You look haggard, Parker," he said. "What's troubling you?"

"It's . . . nothing."

"Everything is something."

"I'm not at liberty to discuss it."

"Would it have anything to do with the execution at Arrowmont Prison this afternoon?"

I blinked. "Why would you surmise that?"

"Logical assumption," Gilloon said. "You are obviously upset, and yet you are a man who lives quietly and suffers no apparent personal problems. You are warden of Arrowmont Prison and the fact of the execution is public knowledge. You customarily come to the inn at eight o'clock, and yet you didn't make your appearance tonight until after eleven."

I said, "I wish I had your mathematical mind, Gilloon."

"Indeed? Why is that?"

"Perhaps then l could find answers where none seem to exist."

"Answers to what?"

A waiter arrived with my Guinness and I took a swallow gratefully.

Gilloon was looking at me with piercing interest. I avoided his one-eyed gaze, knowing I had already said too much. But there was something about Gilloon that demanded confidence. Perhaps he could shed some light on the riddle of Teasdale's disappearance.

"Come now, Parker—answers to what?" he repeated. "Has something happened at the prison?"

And of course I weakened—partly because of frustration and worry, partly because the possibility that I might never learn the secret loomed large and painful. "Yes," I said, "something has happened at the prison. Something incredible, and I mean that literally." I paused to draw a heavy breath. "If I tell you about it, do I have your word that you won't let it go beyond this table?"

"Naturally." Gilloon leaned forward and his good eye glittered with anticipation. "Go on, Parker."

More or less calmly at first, then with increasing agitation as I relived the events, I proceeded to tell Gilloon everything that had transpired at the prison. He listened with attention, not once interrupting. I had never seen him excited prior to that night, but when I had finished, he was fairly squirming. He took off his Scotch cap and ran a hand through his thinning brown hair.

"Fascinating tale," he said.

"Horrifying would be a more appropriate word."

"That too, yes. No wonder you're upset."

"It defies explanation," I said. "And yet there has to be one. I refuse to accept the supernatural implications."

"I wouldn't be so skeptical of the supernatural if I were you, Parker. I've come across a number of things in my travels which could not be satisfactorily explained by man or science."

I stared at him. "Does that mean you believe Teasdale's disappearance was arranged by forces beyond human ken?"

"No, no. I was merely making a considered observation. Have you given me every detail of what happened?"

"I believe so."

"Think it through again—be sure."

Frowning, I reviewed the events once more. And it came to me that I had neglected to mention the brief silvery glimmer which had appeared above the trap in the instant Teasdale plunged through; I had, in fact, forgotten all about it. This time I mentioned it to Gilloon.

"Ah," he said.

"Ah? Does it have significance?"

"Perhaps. Can you be more specific about it?"

"I'm afraid not. It was so brief I took it at the time for an optical illusion."

"You saw no other such glimmers?"

"None."

"How far away from the gallows were you sitting?"

"Approximately forty feet."

"Is the shed equipped with electric lights?"

"No—lanterns."

"I see," Gilloon said meditatively. He seized one of his notebooks, opened it, shielded it from my eyes with his left arm, and began to write with his pencil. He wrote without pause for a good three minutes, before I grew both irritated and anxious.

"Gilloon," I said, "stop that infernal scribbling and tell me what's on your mind."

He gave no indication of having heard me. His pencil continued to scratch against the paper, filling another page. Except for the movement of his right hand and one side of his mouth gnawing at the edge of his mustache, he was as rigid as a block of stone.

"Damn it, Gilloon!"

But it was another ten seconds before the pencil became motionless. He stared at what he had written and then looked up at me. "Parker," he said, "did Arthur Teasdale have a trade?"

The question took me by surprise. "A trade?"

"Yes. What did he do for a living, if anything?"

"What bearing can that have on what's happened?"

"Perhaps a great deal," Gilloon said.

"He worked in a textile mill."

"And there is a textile mill at the prison, correct?"

"Yes."

"Does it stock quantities of silk?"

"Silk? Yes, on occasion. What—?"

I did not finish what I was about to say, for he had shut me out and resumed writing in his notebook. I repressed an oath of exasperation, took a long draught of Guinness to calm myself, and prepared to demand that he tell me what theory he had devised. Before I could do that, however, Gilloon abruptly closed the notebook, slid out of the booth, and loomed over me.

"I'll need to see the execution shed," he said.

"What for?"

"Corroboration of certain facts."

"But—" I stood up hastily. "You've suspicioned a possible answer, that's clear," I said, "though I can't for the life of me see how, on the basis of the information I've given you. What is it?"

"I must see the execution shed," he said firmly. "I will not voice premature speculations."

It touched my mind that the man was a bit mad. After all, I had only known him for a few weeks, and from the first he had been decidedly eccentric in most respects. Still, I had never had cause to question his mental faculties before this, and the aura of self-assurance and confidence he projected was forceful. Because I was so desperate to solve the riddle, I couldn't afford not to indulge, at least for a while, the one man who might be able to provide it.

"Very well," I said, "I'll take you to the prison."

Rain still fell in black torrents—although without thunder and lightning—when I brought my Packard around the last climbing curve onto the promontory. Lanternlight glowed fuzzily in the prison watchtowers, and the bare brick walls had an unpleasant oily sheen. At this hour of night, in the storm, the place seemed forbidding and shrouded in human despair—an atmosphere I had not previously apprehended during the two years I had been its warden. Strange how a brush with the unknown can alter one's perspective and stir the fears that lie at the bottom of one's soul.

Beside me Gilloon did not speak; he sat erect, his hands resting on the notebooks on his lap. I parked in the small lot facing the main gates, and after Gilloon had carefully tucked the notebooks inside his slicker we ran through the downpour to the gates. I gestured to the guard, who nodded beneath the hood of his oilskin, allowed us to enter, and then quickly closed the iron halves behind us and returned to the warmth of the gatehouse. I led Gilloon directly across the compound to the execution shed.

The guards I had posted inside seemed edgy and grateful for company. It was colder now, and despite the fact that all the lanterns were lit it also seemed darker and filled with more restless shadows. But the earlier aura of spiritual menace permeated the air, at least to my sensitivities. If Gilloon noticed it, he gave no indication.

He wasted no time crossing to the gallows and climbing the steps to the platform. I followed him to the trap, which still hung open. Gilloon peered into the cubicle, got onto all fours to squint in the rectangular edges of the opening, and then hoisted the hangman's rope and studied the noose. Finally, with surprising agility, he dropped down inside the cubicle, requesting a lantern which I fetched for him, and spent minutes crawling about with his nose to the floor. He located the thin splinter of wood I had noticed earlier, studied it in the lantern glow, and dropped it into the pocket of his tweed coat.

When he came out through the passageway he wore a look mixed of ferocity and satisfaction. "Stand there a minute, will you?" he said. He hurried over to where the witness chairs were arranged, then called, "In which of these chairs were you sitting during the execution?"

"Fourth one from the left."

Gilloon sat in that chair, produced his notebooks, opened one, and bent over it. I waited with mounting agitation while he committed notes to paper. When he glanced up again, the flickering lanternglow gave his face a spectral cast.

He said, "While Granger placed the noose over Teasdale's head, Hollowell held the prisoner on the trap—is that correct?"

"It is."

"Stand as Hollowell was standing."

I moved to the edge of the opening, turning slightly quarter profile.

"You're certain that was the exact position?"

"Yes."

"Once the trap had been sprung, what did Hollowell do?"

"Moved a few paces away." I demonstrated.

"Did he avert his eyes from the trap?"

"Yes, he did. So did Granger. That's standard procedure."

"Which direction did he face?"

I frowned. "I'm not quite sure," I said. "My attention was on the trap and the rope."

"You're doing admirably, Parker. After Granger threw the trap lever, did he remain standing beside it?"

"Until he had counted off sixty seconds, yes."

"And then?"

"As I told you, he walked to the trap and looked into the cubicle. Again, that is standard procedure for the hangman. When he saw it was empty he uttered a shocked exclamation, went to his knees, and leaned down to see if Teasdale had somehow slipped the noose and fallen or crawled into the passageway."

"At which part of the opening did he go to his knees? Front, rear, one of the sides?"

"The front. But I don't see—"

"Would you mind illustrating?"

I grumbled but did as he asked. Some thirty seconds

passed in silence. Finally I stood and turned, and of course found Gilloon again writing in his notebook. I descended the gallows steps. Gilloon closed the notebook and stood with an air of growing urgency. "Where would Granger be at this hour?" he asked. "Still here at the prison?"

"I doubt it. He came on duty at three and should have gone off again at midnight."

"It's imperative that we find him as soon as possible, Parker. Now that I'm onto the solution of this riddle, there's no time to waste."

"You have solved it?"

"I'm certain I have." He hurried out of the shed.

I felt dazed as we crossed the rain-soaked compound, yet Gilloon's positiveness had infused in me a similar sense of urgency. We entered the administration building and I led the way to Rogers' office, where we found him preparing to depart for the night. When I asked about Granger, Rogers said that he had signed out some fifty minutes earlier, at midnight.

"Where does he live?" Gilloon asked us.

"In Hainesville, I think."

"We must go there immediately, Parker. And we had better take half a dozen well-armed men with us."

"Do you honestly believe that's necessary?"

"I do," Gilloon said. "If we're fortunate, it will help prevent another murder."

The six-mile drive to the village of Hainesville was charged with tension, made even more acute by the muddy roads and the pelting rain. Gilloon stubbornly refused to comment on the way as to whether he believed Granger to be a culpable or innocent party, or as to whether he suspected to find Arthur Teasdale alive—or dead—at Granger's home. There would be time enough later for explanations, he said.

Hunched over the wheel of the Packard, conscious of the two heavily armed prison guards in the rear seat and the head-lamps of Rogers' car following closely behind, I could not help but wonder if I might be making a prize fool of myself. Suppose I had been wrong in my judgment of Gilloon, and he was daft after all? Or a well-meaning fool in his own right? Or worst of all, a hoaxster?

Nevertheless, there was no turning back now. I had long since committed myself. Whatever the outcome, I had placed the fate of my career firmly in the hands of Buckmaster Gilloon.

We entered the outskirts of Hainesville. One of the guards who rode with us lived there, and he directed us down the main street and into a turn just beyond the church. The lane in which Granger lived, he said, was two blocks further up and one block east.

Beside me Gilloon spoke for the first time. "I suggest we park a distance away from Granger's residence, Parker. It won't do to announce our arrival by stopping in front."

I nodded. When I made the turn into the lane I took the Packard onto the verge and doused its lights. Rogers' car drifted in behind, headlamps also winking out. A moment later eight of us stood in a tight group in the roadway, huddling inside our slickers as we peered up the lane.

There were four houses in the block, two on each side, spaced widely apart. The pair on our left, behind which stretched open meadowland, were dark. The furthest of the two on the right was also dark, but the closer one showed light in one of the front windows. Thick smoke curled out of its chimney and was swirled into nothingness by the howling wind. A huge oak shaded the front yard. Across the rear, a copse of swaying pine stood silhouetted against the black sky.

The guard who lived in Hainesville said, "That's

Granger's place, the one showing light."

We left the road and set out across the grassy flatland to the pines, then through them toward Granger's cottage. From a point behind the house, after issuing instructions for the others to wait there, Gilloon, Rogers, and I made our way downward past an old stone well and through a sodden growth of weeds. The sound of the storm muffled our approach as we proceeded single-file, Gilloon tacitly assuming leadership, along the west side of the house to the lighted window.

Gilloon put his head around the frame for the first cautious look inside. Momentarily he stepped back and motioned me to take his place. When I had moved to where I could peer in, I saw Granger standing relaxed before the fireplace, using a poker to prod a blazing fire not wholly composed of logs—something else, a blackened lump already burned beyond recognition, was being consumed there. But he was not alone in the room; a second man stood watching him, an expression of concentrated malevolence on his face and an old hammerless revolver tucked into the waistband of his trousers.

Arthur Teasdale.

I experienced a mixture of relief, rage, and resolve as I moved away to give Rogers his turn. It was obvious that Granger was guilty of complicity in Teasdale's escape—and I had always liked and trusted the man. But I supposed everyone had his price; I may even have had a fleeting wonder as to what my own might be.

After Rogers had his look, the three of us returned to the back yard, where I told him to prepare the rest of the men for a front-and-rear assault on the cottage. Then Gilloon and I took up post in the shadows behind the stone well. Now that my faith in *him,* at least, had been vindicated, I felt an enormous gratitude—but this was hardly the time to express it. Or to ask any of the questions that were racing through my mind. We waited in silence.

In less than four minutes all six of my men had surrounded the house. I could not hear it when those at the front broke in, but the men at the back entered the rear door swiftly. Soon the sound of pistol shots rose above the cry of the storm.

Gilloon and I hastened inside. In the parlor we found Granger sitting on the floor beside the hearth, his head buried in his hands. He had not been injured, nor had any of the guards. Teasdale was lying just beyond the entrance to the center hallway. The front of his shirt was bloody, but he had merely suffered a superficial shoulder wound and was cursing like a madman. He would live to hang again, I remember thinking, in the execution shed at Arrowmont Prison.

Sixty minutes later, after Teasdale had been placed under heavy guard in the prison infirmary and a silent Granger had been locked in a cell, Rogers and Gilloon and I met in my office. Outside, the rain had slackened to a drizzle.

"Now then, Gilloon," I began, "we owe you a great debt, and I acknowledge it here and now. But explanations are long overdue."

He smiled with the air of a man who has just been through an exhilarating experience. "Of course," he said. "Suppose we begin with Hollowell. You're wondering if he was bribed by Teasdale—if he also assisted in the escape. The answer is no: he was an innocent pawn."

"Then why was he killed? Revenge?"

"Not at all. His life was taken—and not at the place where his body was later discovered—so that the escape trick could be worked in the first place. It was one of the primary keys to the plan's success."

"I don't understand," I said. "The escape trick had already been completed when Hollowell was stabbed."

"Ah, but it hadn't," Galloon said. "Hollowell was murdered *before* the execution, sometime between four and five o'clock."

We stared at him. "Gilloon," I said, "Rogers and I and five other witnesses *saw* Hollowell inside the shed—"

"Did you, Parker? The execution shed is lighted by lanterns. On a dark afternoon, during a thunderstorm, visibility is not reliable. And you were some forty feet from him. You saw an average-size man wearing a guard's uniform, with a guard's peaked cap drawn down over his forehead—a man you had no reason to assume was not Hollowell. You took his identity for granted."

"I can't dispute the logic of that," I said. "But if you're right that it wasn't Hollowell, who was it?"

"Teasdale, of course."

"Teasdale! For God's sake, man, if Teasdale assumed the identity of Hollowell, whom did we see carried in as Teasdale?"

"No one," Gilloon said.

My mouth fell open. There was a moment of heavy silence. I broke it finally by exclaiming, "Are you saying we did not see a man hanged at five o'clock this afternoon?"

"Precisely."

"Are you saying we were all victims of some sort of mass hallucination?"

"Certainly not. You saw what you believed to be Arthur Teasdale, just as you saw what you believed to be Hollowell. Again let me remind you: the lighting was poor and you had no reason at the time to suspect deception. But think back, Parker. What actually *did* you see? The shape of a man with a black hood covering his head, supported between two other

149

men. But did you see that figure walk or hear it speak? Did you at any time discern an identifiable part of a human being, such as a hand or an exposed ankle?"

I squeezed my eyes shut for a moment, mentally re-examining the events in the shed. "No," I admitted. "I discerned nothing but the hood and the clothing and the shoes. But I *did* see him struggle at the foot of the gallows, and his body spasm on the trap. How do you explain that?"

"Simply. Like everything else, illusion. At a preconceived time Granger and Teasdale had only to slow their pace and jostle the figure with their own bodies to create the impression that the figure itself was resisting them. Teasdale alone used the same method on the trap."

"If it is your contention that the figure was some sort of dummy, I can't believe it, Gilloon. How could a dummy be made to vanish any more easily than a man?"

"It was not, strictly speaking, a dummy."

"Then what the devil was it?"

Gilloon held up a hand; he appeared to be enjoying himself immensely. "Do you recall my asking if Teasdale had a trade? You responded that he had worked in a textile mill, whereupon I asked if the prison textile mill stocked silk."

"Yes, yes, I recall that."

"Come now, Parker, use your imagination. What is one of the uses of silk—varnished silk?"

"I don't know," I began, but no sooner were the words past my lips than the answer sprang into my mind. "Good Lord—balloons!"

"Exactly."

"The figure we saw was a *balloon?*"

"In effect, yes. It is not difficult to sew and tie off a large piece of silk in the rough shape of a man. When inflated to a malleable state with helium or hydrogen, and seen in poor light from a distance of forty feet or better, while covered entirely by clothing and a hood, and weighted down with a pair of shoes and held tightly by two men—the effect can be maintained.

"The handiwork would have been done by Teasdale in the relative privacy of the death cell. The material was doubtless supplied from the prison textile mill by Granger. Once the sewing and tying had been accomplished, I imagine Granger took the piece out of the prison, varnished it, and returned it later. It need not have been inflated, naturally, until just prior to the execution. As to where the gas was obtained, I would think there would be a cylinder of hydrogen in the prison foundry."

I nodded.

"In any event, between four and five o'clock, when the three of them were alone in the death annex, Teasdale murdered Hollowell with an awl Granger had given him. Granger then transported Hollowell's body behind the stack of lumber a short distance away and probably also returned the gas cylinder to the foundry. The storm would have provided all the shield necessary, though even without it the risk was one worth taking.

"Once Granger and Teasdale had brought the balloon-figure to the gallows, Granger, as hangman, placed the noose carefully around the head. You told me, Parker, that he was the last to examine the noose. While he was doing so he inserted into the fibers at the inner bottom that sharp sliver of wood you found in the trap cubicle. When he drew the noose taut, he made sure the sliver touched the balloon's surface so that when the trap was sprung and the balloon plunged downward the splinter would penetrate the silk. The sound of a balloon deflating is negligible; the storm made it more so. The dancing of the rope, of course, was caused by the escaping air.

"During the ensuing sixty seconds, the balloon completely deflated. There was nothing in the cubicle at that point except a bundle of clothing, silk and shoes. The removal of all but the hood, to complete the trick, was a simple enough matter. You told me how it was done, when you mentioned the silvery glimmer you saw above the trap.

"That glimmer was a brief reflection of lanternlight off a length of thin wire which had been attached to the clothing and to the balloon. Granger concealed the wire in his hand, and played out most of a seven- or eight-foot coil before he threw the trap lever.

"After he had gone to his knees with his back to the witness chairs, he merely opened the front of his duster. No doubt it made something of a bulge, but the attention was focused on other matters. You did notice, Parker—and it was a helpful clue—that Granger appeared to be holding his stomach as if he were about to be ill. What he was actually doing was clutching the bundle so that it would not fall from beneath his duster. Later he hid the bundle among his belongings and transported it out of the prison when he went off duty. It was that bundle we saw burning in the fireplace in his cottage."

"But how did *Teasdale* get out of the prison?"

"The most obvious way imaginable," Gilloon said. "He walked out through the front gates."

"What!"

"Yes. Remember, he was wearing a guard's uniform—supplied by Granger—and there was a storm raging. I noticed when we first arrived tonight that the gateman seemed eager to return to his gatehouse, where it was dry. He scarcely looked at you and did not question me. That being the case, it's obvious that he would not have questioned someone who wore the proper uniform and kept his face averted as he gave

Hollowell's name. The guards had not yet been alerted and the gateman would have no reason to suspect trickery.

"Once out, I suspect Teasdale simply took Granger's car and drove to Hainesville. When Granger himself came off duty, I would guess that he obtained a ride home with another guard, using some pretext to explain the absence of his own vehicle.

"I did not actually *know*, of course, that we would find Teasdale at Granger's place; I made a logical supposition in light of the other facts. Since Granger was the only other man alive who knew how the escape had been worked, I reasoned that an individual of Teasdale's stripe would not care to leave him alive and vulnerable to a confession, no matter what promises he might have made to Granger."

"If Teasdale managed his actual escape that easily, why did he choose to go through all that trickery with the balloon? Why didn't he just murder Hollowell, with Granger's help, and then leave the prison *prior* to the execution, between four and five?"

"Oh, I suppose he thought that the bizarre circumstances surrounding the disappearance of an apparently hanged man would insure him enough time to get clear of this immediate area. If you were confused and baffled, you would not sound an instant alarm, whereas you certainly would have if he had simply disappeared from his cell. Also, the prospect of leaving all of you a legacy of mystery and horror afforded him a warped sense of revenge."

"You're a brilliant man," I told him as I sank back in my chair.

Gilloon shrugged. "This kind of puzzle takes logic rather than brilliance, Parker. As I told you earlier tonight, it isn't always wise to discount the supernatural; but in a case where no clear evidence of the supernatural exits, the answer generally lies in some form of illusion. I've encountered a number of seemingly incredible occurrences, some of which were even more baffling than this one and most of which involved illusion. I expect I'll encounter others in the future as well."

"Why do you say that?"

"One almost seems able after a while to divine places where they will occur," he said matter-of-factly, "and therefore to make oneself available to challenge them."

I blinked at him. "Do you mean you *intuited* something like this would happen at Arrowmont Prison? That you have some sort of prevision?"

"Perhaps. Perhaps not. Perhaps I'm nothing more than a pulp writer who enjoys traveling." He gave me an enigmatic smile and got to his feet clutching his notebooks. "I can't speak for you, Parker," he said, "but I seem to have acquired an intense thirst. You wouldn't happen to know where we might obtain a Guinness at this hour, would you?"

One week later, suddenly and without notice, Gilloon left Arrowmont Village. One day he was there, the next he was not. Where he went I do not know: I neither saw him nor heard of or from him again.

Who and what was Buckmaster Gilloon? Is it possible for one enigma to be attracted and motivated by another enigma? Can that which seems natural and coincidental be the result instead of preternatural forces? Perhaps you can understand now why these questions have plagued me in the sixty years since I knew him. And why I am haunted by that single passage I read by accident in his notebook, the passage which may hold the key to Buckmaster Gilloon:

If a jimbuck stands alone by the sea, on a night when the dark moon sings, how many grains of sand in a single one of his footprints? . . .

Caught in the Act

When I drove around the bend in my driveway at four that Friday afternoon, past the screen of cypress trees, a fat little man in a gray suit was just closing the front door of my house. Surprise made me blink: he was a complete stranger.

He saw the car in that same moment, stiffened, and glanced around in a furtive way, as if looking for an avenue of escape. But there wasn't anywhere for him to go; the house is a split-level, built on the edge of a bluff and flanked by limestone outcroppings and thick vegetation. So he just stood there as I braked to a stop in front of the porch, squared his shoulders, and put on a smile that looked artificial even from a distance of thirty feet.

I got out and ran around to where he was. His smile faded, no doubt because my surprise had given way to anger and because I'm a pretty big man, three inches over six feet, weight 230; I played football for four years in college and I move like the linebacker I was. As for him, he wasn't such-a-much— just a fat little man, soft-looking, with round pink cheeks and shrewd eyes that had nervous apprehension in them now.

"Who are you?" I demanded. "What the hell were you doing in my house?"

"Your house? Ah, then you're James Loomis."

"How did you know that?"

"Your name is on your mailbox, Mr. Loomis."

"What were you doing in my house?"

He looked bewildered. "But I *wasn't* in your house"

"Don't give me that. I saw you closing the door."

"No, sir, you're mistaken. I was just coming *away* from the door. I rang the bell and there was no answer—"

"Listen, you," I said, "don't tell me what I saw or didn't see. My eyesight's just fine. Now I want an explanation."

"There's really nothing to explain," he said. "I represent the Easy-Way Vacuum Cleaner Company and I stopped by to ask if you—"

"Let's see some identification."

He rummaged around in a pocket of his suit coat, came out with a small white business card, and handed it to me. It said he was Morris Tweed, a salesman for the Easy-Way Vacuum Cleaner Company.

"I want to see your driver's license," I said.

"My, ah, driver's license?"

"You heard me. Get it out."

He grew even more nervous. "This is very embarrassing, Mr. Loomis," he said. "You see I, ah, lost my wallet this morning. A very unfortunate—"

I caught onto the front of his coat and bunched the material in my fingers; he made a funny little squeaking sound. I marched him over to the door, reached out with my free hand, and tried the knob. Locked. But that didn't mean anything one way or another; the door has a button you can turn on the inside so you don't have to use a key on your way out.

I looked over at the burglar-alarm panel, and of course the red light was off. Tweed, or whatever his name was, wouldn't have been able to walk out quietly through the front door if the system was operational. And except for my housekeeper, whom I've known for years and who is as trustworthy as they come, I was the only one who had an alarm key.

The fat little man struggled weakly to loosen my grip on his coat. "See here, Mr. Loomis," he said in a half-frightened, half-indignant voice, "you have no right to be rough with me.

I haven't done anything wrong."

"We'll see about that."

I walked him back to the car, got my keys out of the ignition, returned him to the door, and keyed the alarm to the On position. The red light came on, which meant that the system was still functional. I frowned. If it was functional, how had the fat little man got in? Well, there were probably ways for a clever burglar to bypass an alarm system without damaging it; maybe that was the answer.

I shut it off again, unlocked the door, and took him inside. The house had a faint musty smell, the way houses do after they've been shut up for a time; I had been gone eight days, on a planned ten-day business trip to New York, and my housekeeper only comes in once a week. I took him into the living room, sat him down in a chair, and then went over and opened the French doors that led out to the balcony.

On the way back I glanced around the room. Everything was where it should be: the console TV set, the stereo equipment, my small collection of Oriental *objets d'art* on their divider shelves. But my main concern was what was in my study—particularly the confidential records and ledgers locked inside the wall safe.

"All right, you," I said, "take off your coat."

He blinked at me. "My coat? Really, Mr. Loomis, I don't—"

"Take off your coat."

He looked at my face, at the fist I held up in front of his nose, and took off his coat. I went through all the pockets. Sixty-five dollars in a silver money clip, a handkerchief, and a handful of business cards. But that was all; there wasn't anything of mine there, except possibly the money. I shuffled through the business cards. All of them bore the names of different companies and different people, and none of them was a duplicate of the one he had handed me outside.

"Morris Tweed, huh?" I said.

"Those cards were given to me by customers," he said. "*My* cards are in my wallet, all except the one I gave you. And I've already told you that I lost my wallet this morning."

"Sure you did. Empty out your pants pockets."

He sighed, stood up, and transferred three quarters, a dime, a penny, and a keycase to the coffee table. Then he pulled all the pockets inside out. Nothing.

"Turn around," I told him.

When he did that I patted him down the way you see cops do in the movies. Nothing.

"This is all a misunderstanding, Mr. Loomis," he said. "I'm not a thief; I'm a vacuum-cleaner salesman. You've searched me quite thoroughly, you know I don't have anything that belongs to you."

Maybe not—but I had a feeling that said otherwise. There were just too many things about him that didn't add up, and there was the plain fact that I had seen him coming *out* of the house. Call it intuition or whatever: I sensed this fat little man had stolen something from me. Not just come here to steal, because he had obviously been leaving when I arrived. He had something of mine, all right.

But what? And where was it?

I gave him back his coat and watched him put it on. There was a look of impending relief on his face as he scooped up his keys and change; he thought I was going to let him go. Instead I caught hold of his arm. Alarm replaced the relief and he made another of those squeaking noises as I hustled him across the room and down the hall to the smallest of the guest bathrooms, the one with a ventilator in place of a window.

When I pushed him inside he stumbled, caught his balance, and pivoted around to me. "Mr. Loomis, this is outrageous. What do you intend to do with me?"

"That depends. Turn you over to the police, maybe."

"The police? But you can't—"

I took the key out of the inside lock, shut the door on him, and locked it from the outside.

Immediately I went downstairs to my study. The Matisse print was in place and the safe door behind it was closed and locked; I worked the combination, swung the door open. And let out the breath I had been holding: the records and ledgers were there, exactly as I had left them. If those items had fallen into the wrong hands, I would be seriously embarrassed at the least and open to blackmail or possible criminal charges at the worst. Not that I was engaged in anything precisely illegal; it was just that some of the people for whom I set up accounting procedures were involved in certain extra-legal activities.

I looked through the other things in the safe—$2,000 in cash, some jewelry and private papers—and they were all there, untouched. Nothing, it developed, was missing from my desk either. Or from anywhere else in the study.

Frowning, I searched the rest of the house. In the kitchen I found what might have been jimmy marks on the side door. I also found—surprisingly—electrician's tape on the burglar-alarm wires outside, tape which had not been there before I left on my trip and that might have been used to repair a cross-circuiting of the system.

What I did *not* find was anything missing. Absolutely nothing. Every item of value, every item of no value, was in its proper place.

I began to have doubts. Maybe I was wrong after all; maybe this was just a large misunderstanding. And yet, damn it, the fat little man had been in here and had lied about it, he had no identification, he was nervous and furtive, and the burglar alarm and the side door seemed to have been tampered with.

A series of improbable explanations occurred to me. He hadn't actually stolen anything because he hadn't had time; he had broken in here, cased the place, and had been on his way out with the intention of returning later in a car or van. But burglars don't operate that way; they don't make two trips to a house when they can just as easily make one, and they don't walk out the front door in broad daylight without taking *something* with them. Nor for that matter, do they take the time to repair alarm systems they've cross-circuited.

He wasn't a thief but a tramp whose sole reason for breaking in here was to spend a few days at my expense. Only tramps don't wear neat gray suits and they don't have expertise with burglar alarms. And they don't leave your larder full or clean up after themselves.

He wasn't a thief but a private detective, or an edge-of-the-law hireling, or maybe even an assassin; he hadn't come here to steal anything, he had come here to *leave* something— evidence of my extra-legal activities, a bomb or some other sort of death trap. But if there was nothing missing, there was also nothing here that shouldn't be here; I would have found it one way or another if there was, as carefully as I had searched. Besides which, there was already incriminating evidence in my safe, I was very good at my job and got along well with my clients, and I had no personal enemies who could possibly want me dead.

Nothing made sense. The one explanation I kept clinging to didn't make sense. Why would a burglar repair an alarm system before he leaves? How could a thief have stolen something if there wasn't anything missing?

Frustrated and angry, I went back to the guest bathroom and unlocked the door. The fat little man was standing by the sink, drying perspiration from his face with one of my towels. He looked less nervous and apprehensive now; there was a kind of resolve in his expression.

"All right," I said, "come out of there."

He came out, watching me warily with his shrewd eyes. "Are you finally satisfied that I'm not a thief, Mr. Loomis?"

No, I was not satisfied. I considered ordering him to take off his clothes, but that seemed pointless; I had already searched him and there just wasn't anything to look for.

"What were you doing in here?" I said.

"I was *not* in here before you arrived." The indignation was back in his voice. "Now I suggest you let me go on my way. You have no right or reason to hold me here against my will."

I made another fist and rocked it in front of his nose. "Do I have to cuff you around to get the truth?"

He flinched, but only briefly; he had had plenty of time to shore up his courage. "That wouldn't be wise, Mr. Loomis," he said. "I already have grounds for a counter-complaint against you."

"Counter-complaint?"

"For harassment and very probably for kidnapping. Physical violence would only compound a felony charge. I intend to make that counter-complaint if you call the police or if you lay a hand on me."

The anger drained out of me; I felt deflated. Advantage to the fat little man. He had grounds for a counter-complaint, okay—better grounds than I had against him. After all, I *had* forcibly brought him in here and locked him in the bathroom. And a felony charge against me would mean unfavorable publicity, not to mention police attention. In my business I definitely could not afford either of those things.

He had me then, and he knew it. He said stiffly, "May I

leave or not, Mr. Loomis?"

There was nothing I could do. I let him go.

He went at a quick pace through the house, moving the way somebody does in familiar surroundings. I followed him out onto the porch and watched him hurry off down the driveway without once looking back. He was almost running by the time he disappeared behind the screen of cypress trees.

I went back inside and poured myself a double bourbon. I had never felt more frustrated in my life. The fat little man had got away with something of mine; irrationally or not, I felt it with even more conviction than before.

But what could he possibly have taken of any value?

And how could he have taken it?

I found out the next morning.

The doorbell rang at 10:45, while I was working on one of my accounts in the study. When I went out there and answered it I discovered a well-dressed elderly couple, both of whom were beaming and neither of whom I had ever seen before.

"Well," the man said cheerfully, "you must be Mr. Loomis. We're the Parmenters."

"Yes?"

"We just dropped by for another look around," he said. "When we saw your car out front we were hoping it belonged to you. We've been wanting to meet you in person."

I looked at him blankly.

"This is such a delightful place," his wife said. "We can't tell you how happy we are with it."

"Yes, sir," Parmenter agreed, "we knew it was the place for us as soon as your agent showed it to us. And such a reasonable price. Why, we could hardly believe it was only $100,000."

There was a good deal of confusion after that, followed on my part by disbelief, anger, and despair. When I finally got it all sorted out it amounted to this: the Parmenters were supposed to meet here with my "agent" yesterday afternoon, to present him with a $100,000 cashier's check, but couldn't make it at that time; so they had given him the check last night at their current residence, and he in turn had handed them copies of a notarized sales agreement carrying my signatures. The signatures were expert forgeries, of course—but would I be able to *prove* that in a court of law? Would I be able to prove I had not conspired with this bogus real estate agent to defraud the Parmenters of a six-figure sum of money?

Oh, I found out about the fat little man, all right. I found out how clever and audacious he was. And I found out just how wrong I had been—and just how right.

He hadn't stolen anything *from* my house.

He had stolen the whole damned *house*.

Liar's Dice

"Excuse me. Do you play liar's dice?"

I looked over at the man two stools to my right. He was about my age, early forties; average height, average weight, brown hair, medium complexion—really a pretty nondescript sort except for a pleasant and disarming smile. Expensively dressed in an Armani suit and a silk jacquard tie. Drinking white wine. I had never seen him before. Or had I? There was something familiar about him, as if our paths *had* crossed somewhere or other, once or twice.

Not here in Tony's, though. Tony's is a suburban-mall bar that caters to the shopping trade from the big department and grocery stores surrounding it. I stopped in no more than a couple of times a month, usually when Connie asked me to pick up something at Safeway on my way home from San Francisco, occasionally when I had a Saturday errand to run. I knew the few regulars by sight, and it was never very crowded anyway. There were only four patrons at the moment: the nondescript gent and myself on stools, and a young couple in a booth at the rear.

"I do play, as a matter of fact," I said to the fellow. Fairly well too, though I wasn't about to admit that. Liar's dice and I were old acquaintances.

"Would you care to shake for a drink?"

"Well, my usual limit is one . . ."

"For a chit for your next visit, then."

"All right, why not? I feel lucky tonight."

"Do you? Good. I should warn you, I'm very good at the game."

164

"I'm not so bad myself."

"No, I mean I'm *very* good. I seldom lose."

It was the kind of remark that would have nettled me if it had been said with even a modicum of conceit. But he wasn't bragging; he was merely stating a fact, mentioning a special skill of which he felt justifiably proud. So instead of annoying me, his comment made me eager to test him.

We introduced ourselves; his name was Jones. Then I called to Tony for the dice cups. He brought them down, winked at me, said, "No gambling now," and went back to the other end of the bar. Strictly speaking, shaking dice for drinks and/or money is illegal in California. But nobody pays much attention to nuisance laws like that, and most bar owners keep dice cups on hand for their customers. The game stimulates business. I know because I've been involved in some spirited liar's dice tournaments in my time.

Like all good games, liar's dice is fairly simple—at least in its rules. Each player has a cup containing five dice, which he shakes out but keeps covered so only he can see what is showing face up. Then each makes a declaration or "call" in turn: one of a kind, two of a kind, three of a kind, and so on. Each call has to be higher than the previous one, and is based on what the player *knows* is in his hand and what he *thinks* is in the other fellow's—the combined total of the ten dice. He can lie or tell the truth, whichever suits him; but the better liar he is, the better his chances of winning. When one player decides the other is either lying or has simply exceeded the laws of probability, he says, "Come up," and then both reveal their hands. If he's right, he wins.

In addition to being a clever liar, you also need a good grasp of mathematical odds and the ability to "read" your opponent's facial expressions, the inflection in his voice, his body language. The same skills an experienced poker player has to have, which is one reason the game is also called liar's poker.

Jones and I each rolled one die to determine who would go first; mine was the highest. Then we shook all five dice in our cups, banged them down on the bar. What I had showing was four treys and a deuce.

"Your call, Mr. Quint."

"One five," I said.

"One six."

"Two deuces."

"Two fives."

"Three treys."

"Three sixes."

I considered calling him up, since I had no sixes and he would need three showing to win. But I didn't know his methods and I couldn't read him at all. I decided to keep playing.

"Four treys."

"Five treys."

"Six treys."

Jones smiled and said, "Come up." And he had just one trey (and no sixes). I'd called six treys and there were only five in our combined hands; he was the winner.

"So much for feeling lucky," I said, and signaled Tony to bring another white wine for Mr. Jones. On impulse I decided a second Manhattan wouldn't hurt me and ordered that too.

Jones said, "Shall we play again?"

"Two drinks is definitely my limit."

"For dimes, then? Nickels or pennies, if you prefer."

"Oh, I don't know . . ."

"You're a good player, Mr. Quint, and I don't often find someone who can challenge me. Besides, I have a passion as well as an affinity for liar's dice. Won't you indulge me?"

I didn't see any harm in it. If he'd wanted to play for larger stakes, even a dollar a hand, I might have taken him for a hustler despite his Armani suit and silk tie. But how much could you win or lose playing for a nickel or a dime a hand? So I said, "Your call first this time," and picked up my dice cup.

We played for better than half an hour. And Jones wasn't just good; he was uncanny. Out of nearly twenty-five hands, I won two—*two*. You could chalk up some of the disparity to luck, but not enough to change the fact that his skill was remarkable. Certainly he was the best I'd ever locked horns with. I would have backed him in a tournament anywhere, anytime.

He was a good winner, too: no gloating or chiding. And a good listener, the sort who seems genuinely (if superficially) interested in other people. I'm not often gregarious, especially with strangers, but I found myself opening up to Jones—and this in spite of him beating the pants off me the whole time.

I told him about Connie, how we met and the second honeymoon trip we'd taken to Lake Louise three years ago and what we were planning for our twentieth wedding anniversary in August. I told him about Lisa, who was eighteen and a freshman studying film at UCLA. I told him about Kevin, sixteen now and captain of his high school baseball team, and the five-hit, two home run game he'd had last week. I told him what it was like working as a design engineer for one of the largest engineering firms in the country, the nagging dissatisfaction and the desire to be my own boss someday, when I had enough money saved so I could afford to take the risk. I told him about remodeling our home, the boat I was thinking of buying, the fact that I'd always wanted to try hang-gliding but never had the courage.

Lord knows what else I might have told him if I hadn't noticed the polite but faintly bored expression on his face, as if I were imparting facts he already knew. It made me realize just how much I'd been nattering on, and embarrassed me a bit. I've never liked people who talk incessantly about themselves, as though they're the focal point of the entire universe. I can be a good listener myself; and for all I knew, Jones was a lot more interesting than bland Jeff Quint.

I said, "Well, that's more than enough about me. It's your turn, Jones. Tell me about yourself."

"If you like, Mr. Quint." Still very formal. I'd told him a couple of times to call me Jeff but he wouldn't do it. Now that I thought about it, he hadn't mentioned his own first name.

"What is it you do?"

He laid his dice cup to one side. I was relieved to see that; I'd had enough of losing but I hadn't wanted to be the one to quit. And it was getting late—dark outside already—and Connie would be wondering where I was. A few minutes of listening to the story of his life, I thought, just to be polite, and then—

"To begin with," Jones was saying, "I travel."

"Sales job?"

"No. I travel because I enjoy traveling. And because I can afford it. I have independent means."

"Lucky you. In more ways than one."

"Yes."

"Europe, the South Pacific—all the exotic places?"

"Actually, no. I prefer the U.S."

"Any particular part?"

"Wherever my fancy leads me."

"Hard to imagine anyone's fancy leading him to Bayport," I said. "You have friends or relatives here?"

"No, I have business in Bayport."

"Business? I thought you said you didn't need to work. . . ."

"Independent means, Mr. Quint. That doesn't preclude a purpose, a direction in one's life."

"You do have a profession, then?"

"You might say that. A profession and a hobby combined."

"Lucky you," I said again. "What is it?"

"I kill people," he said.

I thought I'd misheard him. "You . . . what?"

"I kill people."

"Good God. Is that supposed to be a joke?"

"Not at all. I'm quite serious."

"What do you mean, you *kill* people?"

"Just what I said."

"Are you trying to tell me you're . . . some kind of paid assassin?"

"Not at all. I've never killed anyone for money."

"Then why . . . ?"

"Can't you guess?"

"No, I can't guess. I don't want to guess."

"Call it personal satisfaction," he said.

"What people? Who?"

"No one in particular," Jones said. "My selection process is completely random. I'm very good at it too. I've been killing people for . . . let's see, nine and a half years now. Eighteen victims in thirteen states. And, oh yes, Puerto Rico—one in Puerto Rico. I don't mind saying that I've never even come close to being caught."

I stared at him. My mouth was open; I knew it but I couldn't seem to unlock my jaw. I felt as if reality had suddenly slipped away from me, as if Tony had dropped some sort of mind-altering drug into my second Manhattan and it was just now taking effect. Jones and I were still sitting companionably, on adjacent stools now, he smiling and speaking in the same low, friendly voice. At the other end of the bar Tony was slicing lemons and limes into wedges. Three of the booths were occupied now, with people laughing and enjoying themselves. Everything was just as it had been two minutes ago, except that instead of me telling Jones about being a dissatisfied design engineer, he was calmly telling me he was a serial murderer.

I got my mouth shut finally, just long enough to swallow into a dry throat. Then I said, "You're crazy, Jones. You must be insane."

"Hardly, Mr. Quint. I'm as sane as you are."

"I don't believe you killed eighteen people."

"Nineteen," he said. "Soon to be twenty."

"Twenty? You mean . . . someone in Bayport?"

"Right here in Bayport."

"You expect me to believe you intend to pick somebody at random and just . . . murder him in cold blood?"

"Oh no, there's more to it than that. Much more."

"More?" I said blankly.

"I choose a person at random, yes, but carefully. Very carefully. I study my target, follow him as he goes about his daily business, learn everything I can about him down to the minutest detail. Then the cat and mouse begins. I don't murder him right away; that wouldn't give sufficient, ah, satisfaction. I wait . . . observe . . . plan. Perhaps, for added spice, I reveal myself to him. I might even be so bold as to tell him to his face that he's my next victim."

My scalp began to crawl.

"Days, weeks . . . then, when the victim least expects it, a gunshot, a push out of nowhere in front of an oncoming car, a hypodermic filled with digitalin and jabbed into the body on a crowded street, simulating heart failure. There are many ways to kill a man. Did you ever stop to consider just how many different ways there are?"

"You . . . you're not saying—"

"What, Mr. Quint? That I've chosen *you?*"

"Jones, for God's sake!"

"But I have," he said. "You are to be number twenty."

One of my hands jerked upward, struck his arm. Involuntary spasm; I'm not a violent man. He didn't even flinch. I pulled my hand back, saw that it was shaking, and clutched the fingers tight around the beveled edge of the bar.

Jones took a sip of wine. Then he smiled—and winked at me.

"Or then again," he said, "I might be lying."

". . . What?"

"Everything I've just told you might be a lie. I might not have killed nineteen people over the past nine and a half years; I might not have killed anyone, ever."

"I don't . . . I don't know what you—"

"Or I might have told you part of the truth . . . that's another possibility, isn't it? Part fact, part fiction. But in that case, which is which? And to what degree? Am I a deadly threat to you, or am I nothing more than a man in a bar playing a game?"

"Game? What kind of sick—"

"The same one we've been playing all along. Liar's dice."

"Liar's dice?"

"My own special version," he said, "developed and refined through years of practice. The perfect form of the game, if I do say so myself—exciting, unpredictable, filled with intrigue and mortal danger for myself as well as my opponent."

I shook my head. My mind was a seething muddle; I couldn't seem to fully grasp what he was saying.

"I don't know any more than you do at this moment how you'll play your part of the hand, Mr. Quint. That's where the excitement and the danger lies. Will you treat what I've said as you would a bluff? Can you afford to take that risk? Or will you act on the assumption that I've told the monstrous truth, or at least part of it?"

"Damn you . . ." Weak and ineffectual words, even in my own ears.

"And if you do believe me," he said, "what course of action will you take? Attack me before I can harm you, attempt to kill me . . . here and now in this public place, perhaps, in front of witnesses who will swear the attack was unprovoked? Try to follow me when I leave, attack me elsewhere? I might well be armed, and an excellent shot with a handgun. Go to the police . . . with a wild-sounding and unsubstantiated story that they surely wouldn't believe? Hire a detective to track me down? Attempt to track me down yourself? Jones isn't my real name, of course, and I've taken precautions against anyone finding out my true identity. Arm yourself and remain on guard until, if and when, I make a move against you? How long could you live under such intense pressure without making a fatal mistake?"

He paused dramatically. "Or—and this is the most exciting prospect of all, the one I hope you choose—will you mount a clever counterattack, composed of lies and deceptions of your own devising? Can you actually hope to beat me at my own game? Do you dare to try?"

He adjusted the knot in his tie with quick, deft movements, smiling at me in the back-bar mirror—not the same pleasant smile as before. This one had shark's teeth in it. "Whatever you do, I'll know about it soon afterward. I'll be waiting . . . watching . . . and I'll know. And then it will be my turn again."

He slid off his stool, stood poised behind me. I just sat there; it was as if I were paralyzed.

"Your call, Mr. Quint," he said. And he was gone into the night.

The Dispatching of George Ferris

Mrs. Beresford and Mrs. Lenhart were sitting together in the parlor, knitting and discussing recipes for fruit cobbler, when Mr. Pascotti came hurrying in. "There's big news," he said. "Mr. Ferris is dead."

A gleam came into Mrs. Beresford's eyes. She looked at Mrs. Lenhart, noted a similar gleam, and said to Mr. Pascotti, "You did say dead, didn't you?"

"Dead. Murdered."

"Murdered? Are you sure?"

"Well," Mr. Pascotti said, "he's lying on the floor of his room all over blood, with a big knife sticking in his chest. What else would you call it?"

"Oh, yes," Mrs. Lenhart agreed. "Definitely murder."

Mrs. Beresford laid down her knitting and folded her hands across her shelflike bosom. "How did you happen to find him, Mr. Pascotti?"

"By accident. I was on my way down to the john—"

"Lavatory," Mrs. Lenhart said.

"—and I noticed his door was open. He never leaves his door open, not when he's here and not when he's not here. So I'm a good neighbor. I peeked inside to see if something was wrong, and there he was, all over blood."

Mrs. Beresford did some reflecting. George Ferris had been a resident of their roominghouse for six months, during which time he had managed to create havoc in what had formerly been a peaceful and pleasant environment. She and the other residents had complained to the landlord, but the landlord lived elsewhere and chose not to give credence to what he termed "petty differences among neighbors." He also seemed to like Mr. Ferris, with whom he had had minor business dealings before Ferris' retirement and who he considered to possess a sparkling sense of humor. This flaw in his judgment of human nature made him a minority of one, but in this case the minority's opinion was law.

The problem with Mr. Ferris was that he had been a practical joker. Not just an occasional practical joker; oh, no. A constant, unending, remorseless practical joker. A *Practical Joker* with capitals and in italics. Sugar in the salt shaker; ground black pepper in the tea. Softboiled eggs substituted for hardboiled eggs. Kitchen cleanser substituted for denture powder. Four white rats let loose in the dining room during supper. Photographs of naked ladies pasted inside old Mr. Tipton's *Natural History* magazine. Whoopee cushions, water glasses that dribbled, fuzzy spiders and rubber-legged centipedes all over the walls and furniture. These and a hundred other indignities—a deluge, an avalanche of witless and childish pranks.

Was it any wonder, Mrs. Beresford thought, that somebody had finally done him in? No, it was not. The dispatching of George Ferris, the joker, was in fact an act of great mercy.

"Who could have done it?" Mrs. Lenhart asked after a time.

"Anybody who lives here," Mr. Pascotti said. "Anybody who ever spent ten minutes with that lunatic."

"You don't suppose it was an intruder?"

"Who would want to intrude in this place? No, my guess is it was one of us."

"You don't mean one of *us?*"

"What, you or Mrs. Beresford? Nice widow ladies like you? The thought never crossed my mind, believe me."

"Why, thank you, Mr. Pascotti."

"For what?"

"The compliment. You said we were nice widow ladies."

Mr. Pascotti, who had been a bachelor for nearly seven decades, looked somewhat uncomfortable. "You don't have to worry—the police won't suspect you, either. They'd have to be crazy. Policemen today are funny, but they're not crazy."

"They might suspect you, though," Mrs. Beresford said.

"Me? That's ridiculous. All I did was find him on my way to the john—"

"Lavatory," Mrs. Lenhart said.

"All I did was find him. I didn't make him all over blood."

"But they might think you did," Mrs. Beresford said.

"Not a chance. Ferris was ten years younger than me and I've got arthritis so bad I can't even knock loud on a door. So how could I stick a big knife in his chest?"

Mrs. Lenhart adjusted the drape of her shawl. "You know, I really can't imagine anybody here doing such a thing. Can you, Irma?"

"As a matter of fact," Mrs. Beresford said, "I can. We all have hidden strengths and capacities, but we don't realize it until we're driven to the point of having to use them."

"That's very profound."

"Sure it is," Mr. Pascotti said. "It's also true."

"Oh, I'm sure it is. But I still prefer to think it was an intruder who sent Mr. Ferris on to his reward, whatever that may be."

Mr. Pascotti gestured toward the parlor windows and the sunshine streaming in through them. "It's broad daylight," he said. "Do intruders intrude in broad daylight?"

"Sometimes they do," Mrs. Lenhart said. "Remember last year, when the police questioned everybody about strangers in the neighborhood? There was a series of daylight burglaries right over on Hawthorn Boulevard."

"So it could have been an intruder, I'll admit it. We'll tell the police that's what we think. Why should any of us have to suffer for making that lunatic dead?"

"Isn't it time we did?" Mrs. Beresford asked.

"Did? Did what?"

"Tell the police what we think. After we tell them Mr. Ferris is lying up in his room with a knife in his chest."

"You're right," Mr. Pascotti said, "it is time. Past time. A warm day like this, things happen to dead bodies after a while."

He turned and started over to the telephone. But before he got to it there was a sudden eruption of noise from out in the front hallway. At first it sounded to Mrs. Beresford like a series of odd snorts, wheezes, coughs, and gasps. When all these sounds coalesced into a recognizable bellow, however, she realized that what she was hearing was wild laughter.

Then George Ferris walked into the room.

He was wearing an old sweatshirt and a pair of old dungarees, both of which were, as Mr. Pascotti had said, all over blood. In his left hand he carried a wicked-looking and also very bloody knife. His chubby face was contorted into an expression of mirth bordering on ecstasy and he was laughing so hard that tears flowed down both cheeks.

Mrs. Beresford stared at him with her mouth open. So did Mrs. Lenhart and Mr. Pascotti. Ferris looked back at each of them and what he saw sent him into even greater convulsions.

The noise lasted for fifteen seconds or so, subsided into more snorts, wheezes, and gasps, and finally ceased altogether. Ferris wiped his damp face and got his breathing under control. Then he pointed to the crimson stains on his clothing. "Chicken blood," he said. He pointed to the weapon clutched in his left hand. "Trick knife," he said.

"A joke," Mr. Pascotti said. "It was all a joke."

"Another joke," Mrs. Lenhart said.

"Another indignity," Mrs. Beresford said.

"And you fell for it," Ferris reminded them. "Oh, boy, did you fall for it! You should have seen your faces when I walked in." He began to cackle again. "My best one yet," he said, "no question about it. My best one *ever*. Why, by golly, I don't think I'll live to pull off a better one."

Mrs. Beresford looked at Mrs. Lenhart. Then she looked at Mr. Pascotti. Then she picked up one of her knitting needles and looked at the pudgy joker across its sharp glittering point.

"Neither do we, Mr. Ferris," she said. "Neither do we."

The Big Bite

A "Nameless Detective" Story

I laid a red queen on a black king, glanced up at Jay Cohalan through the open door of his office. He was pacing again, back and forth in front of his desk, his hands in constant restless motion at his sides. The office was carpeted; his footfalls made no sound. There was no discernible sound anywhere except for the faint snap and slap when I turned over a card and put it down. An office building at night is one of the quietest places there is. Eerily so, if you spend enough time listening to the silence.

Trey. Nine of diamonds. Deuce. Jack of spades. I was marrying the jack to the red queen when Cohalan quit pacing and came over to stand in the doorway. He watched me for a time, his hands still doing scoop-shovel maneuvers—a big man in his late thirties, handsome except for a weak chin, a little sweaty and disheveled now.

"How can you just sit there playing cards?" he said.

There were several answers to that. Years of stakeouts and dull routine. We'd only been waiting about two hours. The money, fifty thousand in fifties and hundreds, didn't belong to me. I wasn't worried, upset, or afraid that something might go wrong. I passed on all of those and settled instead for a neutral response: "Solitaire's good for waiting. Keeps your mind off the clock."

"It's after seven. Why the hell doesn't he call?"

"You know the answer to that. He wants you to sweat."

"Sadistic bastard."

"Blackmail's that kind of game," I said. "Torture the victim, bend his will to yours."

"Game. My God." Cohalan came out into the anteroom and began to pace around there, in front of his secretary's desk where I was sitting. "It's driving me crazy, trying to figure out who he is, how he found out about my past. Not a hint, any of the times I talked to him. But he knows everything, every damn detail."

"You'll have the answers before long."

"Yeah." He stopped abruptly, leaned toward me. "Listen, this has to be the end of it. You've *got* to stay with him, see to it he's arrested. I can't take any more."

"I'll do my job, Mr. Cohalan, don't worry."

"Fifty thousand dollars. I almost had a heart attack when he told me that was how much he wanted this time. The last payment, he said. What a crock. He'd come back for more some day. I know it, Carolyn knows it, you know it." Pacing again. "Poor Carolyn. Highstrung, emotional . . . it's been even harder on her. She wanted me to go to the police this time, did I tell you that?"

"You told me."

"I should have, I guess. Now I've got to pay a middleman for what I could've had for nothing . . . no offense."

"None taken."

"I just couldn't bring myself to do it, walk into the Hall of Justice and confess everything to a cop. It was hard enough letting Carolyn talk me into hiring a private detective. That trouble when I was a kid . . . it's a criminal offense, I could still be prosecuted for it. And it's liable to cost me my job if it comes out. I went through hell telling Carolyn in the beginning, and I didn't go into all the sordid details. With you, either. The police . . . no. I know that bastard will probably spill the whole story when he's arrested, try to drag me down with him, but still . . . I keep hoping he won't. You understand?"

"I understand," I said.

"I shouldn't've paid him when he crawled out of the woodwork eight months ago. I know that now. But back then it seemed like the only way to keep from ruining my life. Carolyn thought so, too. If I hadn't started paying him, half of her inheritance wouldn't already be gone . . ." He let the rest of it trail off, paced in bitter silence for a time, and started up again. "I hated taking money from her—*hated* it, no matter how much she insisted it belongs to both of us. And I hate myself for doing it, almost as much as I hate him. Blackmail's the worst goddamn crime there is short of murder."

"Not the worst," I said, "but bad enough."

"This *has* to be the end of it. The fifty thousand in there . . . it's the last of her inheritance, our savings. If that son of a bitch gets away with it, we'll be wiped out. You can't let that happen."

I didn't say anything. We'd been through all this before, more than once.

Cohalan let the silence resettle. Then, as I shuffled the cards for a new hand, "This job of mine, you'd think it pays pretty well, wouldn't you? My own office, secretary, executive title, expense account . . . looks good and sounds good, but it's a frigging dead end. Junior account executive stuck in corporate middle management—that's all I am or ever will be. Sixty thousand a year gross. And Carolyn makes twenty-five teaching. Eighty-five thousand for two people, no kids, that seems like plenty but it's not, not these days. Taxes, high cost of living, you have to scrimp to put anything away. And then some stupid mistake you made when you were a kid comes back to haunt you, drains your future along with your bank account, preys on your mind so you can't sleep, can barely do your work . . . you see what I mean? But I didn't think I had a choice at first, I was afraid of losing this crappy job, going to prison. Caught between a rock and a hard place. I still feel that way but now I don't care, I just want that scum to get what's coming to him . . ."

Repetitious babbling caused by his anxiety. His mouth had a wet look and his eyes kept jumping from me to other points in the room.

I said, "Why don't you sit down?"

"I can't sit. My nerves are shot."

"Take a few deep breaths before you start to hyperventilate."

"Listen, don't tell me what—"

The telephone on his desk went off.

The sudden clamor jerked him half around, as if with an electric shock. In the quiet that followed the first ring I could hear the harsh rasp of his breathing. He looked back at me as the bell sounded again. I was on my feet too by then.

I said, "Go ahead, answer it. Keep your head."

He went into his office, picked up just after the third ring. I timed the lifting of the extension to coincide, so there wouldn't be a second click on the open line.

"Yes," he said, "Cohalan."

"You know who this is." The voice was harsh, muffled, indistinctively male. "You got the fifty thousand?"

"I told you I would. The last payment, you promised me . . ."

"Yeah, the last one."

"Where this time?"

"Golden Gate Park. Kennedy Drive, in front of the buffalo pen. Put it in the trash barrel beside the bench there."

Cohalan was watching me through the open doorway. I

shook my head at him. He said into the phone, "Can't we make it someplace else? There might be people around . . ."

"Not at nine p.m."

"Nine? But it's only a little after seven now—"

"Nine sharp. Be there with the cash."

The line went dead.

I cradled the extension. Cohalan was still standing alongside his desk, hanging onto the receiver the way a drowning man might hang onto a lifeline, when I went into his office. I said, "Put it down, Mr. Cohalan."

"What? Oh, yes . . ." He lowered the receiver. "Christ," he said then.

"You all right?"

His head bobbed up and down a couple of times. He ran a hand over his face and then swung away to where his briefcase lay. The fifty thousand was in there; he'd shown it to me when I first arrived. He picked the case up, set it down again. Rubbed his face another time.

"Maybe I *shouldn't* risk the money," he said.

He wasn't talking to me so I didn't answer.

"I could leave it right here where it'll be safe. Put a phone book or something in for weight." He sank into his desk chair; popped up again like a jack-in-the-box. He was wired so tight I could almost hear him humming. "No, what's the matter with me, that won't work. I'm not thinking straight. He might open the case in the park. There's no telling what he'd do if the money's not there. And he's got to have it in his possession when the police come."

"That's why I insisted we mark some of the bills."

"Yes, right, I remember. Proof of extortion. All right, but for God's sake don't let him get away with it."

"He won't get away with it."

Another jerky nod. "When're you leaving?"

"Right now. You stay put until at least eight-thirty. It won't take you more than twenty minutes to get out to the park."

"I'm not sure I can get through another hour of waiting around here."

"Keep telling yourself it'll be over soon. Calm down. The state you're in now, you shouldn't even be behind the wheel."

"I'll be okay."

"Come straight back here after you make the drop. You'll hear from me as soon as I have anything to report."

"Just don't make me wait too long," Cohalan said. And then, again and to himself, "I'll be okay."

Cohalan's office building was on Kearney, not far from where Kerry works at the Bates and Carpenter ad agency on lower Geary. She was on my mind as I drove down to Geary and turned west toward the park; my thoughts prompted me to lift the car phone and call the condo. No answer. Like me, she puts in a lot of overtime night work. A wonder we manage to spend as much time together as we do.

I tried her private number at B & C and got her voice mail. In transit, probably, the same as I was. Headlights crossing the dark city. Urban night riders. Except that she was going home and I was on my way to nail a shakedown artist for a paying client.

That started me thinking about the kind of work I do. One of the downsides of urban night riding is that it gives vent to sometimes broody self-analysis. Skip traces, insurance claims investigations, employee background checks—they're the meat of my business. There used to be some challenge to jobs like that, some creative maneuvering required, but nowadays it's little more than routine legwork (mine) and a lot of computer time (Tamara Corbin, my technowhiz assistant). I don't get to use my head as much as I once did. My problem, in Tamara's Generation X opinion, was that I was a "retro dick" pining away for the old days and old ways. True enough; I never have adapted well to change. The detective racket just isn't as satisfying or stimulating after thirty-plus years and with a new set of rules.

Every now and then, though, a case comes along that stirs the juices—one with some spark and sizzle and a much higher satisfaction level than the run of the mill stuff. I live for cases like that; they're what keep me from packing it in, taking an early retirement. They usually involve a felony of some sort, and sometimes a whisper if not a shout of danger, and allow me to use my full complement of functional brain cells. This Cohalan case, for instance. This one I liked, because shakedown artists are high on my list of worthless lowlives and I enjoy hell out of taking one down.

Yeah, this one I liked a whole lot.

Golden Gate Park has plenty of daytime attractions—museums, tiny lakes, rolling lawns, windmills, an arboretum—but on a foggy November night it's a mostly empty green place to pass through on your way to somewhere else. Mostly empty because it does have its night denizens: homeless squatters, not all of whom are harmless or drug-free, and predators on the prowl in its sprawling acres of shadows and nightshapes. On a night like this it also has an atmosphere of lonely isolation, the fog hiding the city lights and turning streetlamps and passing headlights into surreal blurs.

The buffalo enclosure is at the westward end, less than a mile from the ocean—the least-traveled section of the park at night. There were no cars in the vicinity, moving or parked, when I came down Kennedy Drive. My lights picked out the fence on the north side, the rolling pastureland beyond; the trash barrel and bench were about halfway along, at the edge of the bicycle path that parallels the road. I drove past there, looking for a place to park and wait. I didn't want to sit on Kennedy; a lone car close to the drop point would be too conspicuous. I had to do this right. If anything did not seem kosher, the whole thing might fail to go off the way it was supposed to.

The perfect spot came up fifty yards or so from the trash barrel, opposite the buffaloes' feeding corral—a narrow road that leads to Anglers Lodge where the city maintains casting pools for fly fishermen to practice on. Nobody was likely to go up there at night, and trees and shrubbery bordered one side, the shadows in close to them thick and clotted. Kennedy Drive was still empty in both directions; I cut in past the Anglers Lodge sign and drove up the road until I found a place where I could turn around. Then I shut off my lights, made the U-turn, and coasted back down into the heavy shadows. From there I could see the drop point clearly enough, even with the low-riding fog. I shut off the engine, slumped down on the seat with my back against the door.

No detective, public or private, likes stakeouts. Dull, boring, dead time that can be a literal pain in the ass if it goes on long enough. This one wasn't too bad because it was short, only about an hour, but time lagged and crawled just the same. Now and then a car drifted by, its lights reflecting off rather than boring through the wall of mist. The ones heading west may have been able to see my car briefly in dark silhouette as they passed, but none of them happened to be a police patrol and nobody else was curious enough or venal enough to stop and investigate.

The luminous dial on my watch showed five minutes to nine when Cohalan showed up. Predictably early because he was so anxious to get it over with. He came down Kennedy too fast for the conditions; I heard the squeal of brakes as he swung over and rocked to a stop near the trash barrel. I watched the shape of him get out and run across the path to make the drop and then run back. Ten seconds later his car hissed past where I was hidden, again going too fast, and was gone.

Nine o'clock.

Nine oh five.

Nine oh eight.

Headlights probed past, this set heading east, the car low-slung and smallish. It rolled along slowly until it was opposite the barrel, then veered sharply across the road and slid to a crooked stop with its brake lights flashing blood red. I sat up straighter, put my hand on the ignition key. The door opened without a light coming on inside and the driver jumped out in a hurry, bulky and indistinct in a heavy coat and some kind of head covering; ran to the barrel, scooped out the briefcase, raced back and hurled it inside; hopped in after it and took off. Fast, even faster than Cohalan had been driving, the car's rear end fishtailing a little as the tires fought for traction on the slick pavement.

I was out on Kennedy and in pursuit within seconds. No way I could drive in the fog-laden darkness without putting on my lights, and in the far reach of the beams I could see the other car a hundred yards or so ahead. But even when I accelerated I couldn't get close enough to read the license plate.

Where the Drive forks on the east end of the buffalo enclosure, the sports job made a tight-angle left turn, brake lights flashing again, headlights yawing as the driver fought for control. Looping around Spreckels Lake to quit the park on 36th Avenue. I took the turn at about half the speed, but I still had it in sight when it made a sliding right through a red light on Fulton, narrowly missing an oncoming car, and disappeared

187

to the east. I wasn't even trying to keep up any longer. If I continued pursuit, somebody—an innocent party—was liable to get hurt or killed. That was the last thing I wanted to happen. High-speed car chases are for damn fools and the makers of trite Hollywood films.

I pulled over near the Fulton intersection, still inside the park, and used the car phone to call my client.

Cohalan threw a fit when I told him what had happened. He called me all kinds of names, the least offensive of which was "incompetent idiot." I just let him rant. There were no excuses to be made and no point in wasting my own breath.

He ran out of abuse finally and segued into lament. "What am I going to do now? What am I going to tell Carolyn? All our savings gone and I still don't have any idea who that blackmailing bastard is. What if he comes back for more? We couldn't even sell the house, there's hardly any equity . . ."

Pretty soon he ran down there too. I waited through about five seconds of dead air. Then, "All right," followed by a heavy sigh. "But don't expect me to pay your bill. You can damn well sue me and you can't get blood out of a turnip." And he banged the receiver in my ear.

Some Cohalan. Some piece of work.

The apartment building was on Locust Street a half block off California, close to the Presidio. Built in the twenties, judging by its ornate facade; once somebody's modestly affluent private home, long ago cut up into three floors of studios and one-bedroom apartments. It had no garage, forcing its tenants—like most of those in the neighboring buildings— into street parking. There wasn't a legal space to be had on that block, or in the next, or anywhere in the vicinity. Back on

California, I slotted my car into a bus zone. If I got a ticket I got a ticket.

Not much chance I'd need a weapon for the rest of it, but sometimes trouble comes when you least expect it. So I unclipped the .38 Colt Bodyguard from under the dash, slipped it into my coat pocket before I got out for the walk down Locust.

The building had a tiny foyer with the usual bank of mailboxes. I found the button for 2-C, leaned on it. This was the ticklish part; I was banking on the fact that one voice sounds pretty much like another over an intercom. Turned out not to be an issue at all: The squawk box stayed silent and the door release buzzed instead, almost immediately. Confident. Arrogant. Or just plain stupid.

I pushed inside, smiling a little, cynically, and climbed the stairs to the second floor. 2-C was the first apartment on the right. The door opened just as I got to it, and Annette Byers put her head out and said with excitement in her voice, "You made really good—"

The rest of it snapped off when she got a look at me; the excitement gave way to confusion, froze her in the half-open doorway. I had time to move up on her, wedge my shoulder against the door before she could decide to jump back and slam it in my face. She let out a little bleat and tried to kick me as I crowded her inside. I caught her arms, gave her a shove to get clear of her. Then I nudged the door closed with my heel.

"I'll start screaming," she said. Shaky bravado, the kind without anything to back it up. Her eyes were frightened now. "These walls are paper thin and I've got a neighbor who's a cop."

That last part was a lie. I said, "Go ahead. Be my guest."

"Who the hell do you think you are—"

"We both know who I am, Ms. Byers. And why I'm here.

The reason's on the table over there."

In spite of herself she glanced to her left. The apartment was a studio and the kitchenette and dining area were over that way. The briefcase sat on the dinette table, its lid raised. I couldn't see inside from where I was, but then I didn't need to.

"I don't know what you're talking about," she said.

She hadn't been back long; she still wore the heavy coat and the head covering, a wool stocking cap that completely hid her blond hair. Her cheeks were flushed—the cold night, money lust, now fear. She was attractive enough in a too-ripe way, intelligent enough to hold down a job with a downtown travel service, and immoral enough to have been in trouble with the San Francisco police before this. She was twenty-three, divorced, and evidently a crankhead: she'd been arrested once for possession and once for trying to sell a small quantity of methamphetamine to an undercover cop.

"Counting the cash, right?" I said.

". . . What?"

"What you were doing when I rang the bell. Fifty thousand in fifties and hundreds. It's all there, according to plan."

"I don't know what you're talking about."

"You said that already."

I moved a little to get a better scan of the studio. Her phone was on a breakfast bar that separated the kitchenette from the living room, one of those cordless types with a built-in answering machine. The gadget beside it was clearly a portable cassette player. She hadn't bothered to put it away before she went out; there'd been no reason to, or so she'd have thought then. The tape would still be inside.

I looked at her again. "I've got to admit, you're a pretty good driver. Reckless as hell, though, the way you went flying out of the park on a red light. You came close to a collision with another car."

190

"I don't know what—" She broke off and backed away a couple of paces, her hand rubbing the side of her face, her tongue making little flicks between her lips. It was sinking in now, how it had all gone wrong, how much trouble she was in. "You couldn't have followed me. I *know* you didn't."

"That's right, I couldn't and I didn't."

"Then how—?"

"Think about it. You'll figure it out."

A little silence. And, "Oh God, you knew about me all along."

"About you, the plan, everything."

"How? How could you? I don't—"

The downstairs bell made a sudden racket.

Her gaze jerked past me toward the intercom unit next to the door. She sucked in her lower lip, began to gnaw on it.

"You know who it is," I said. "Don't use the intercom, just the door release."

She did what I told her, moving slowly. I went the other way, first to the breakfast bar where I popped the tape out of the cassette player and slipped it into my pocket, then to the dinette table. I lowered the lid on the briefcase, snapped the catches. I had the case in my hand when she turned to face me again.

She said, "What're you going to do with the money?"

"Give it back to its rightful owner."

"Jay. It belongs to him."

I didn't say anything to that.

"You better not try to keep it for yourself," she said. "You don't have any right to that money . . ."

"You dumb kid," I said disgustedly, "neither do you."

She quit looking at me. When she started to open the door I told her no, wait for his knock. She stood with her back to me, shoulders hunched. She was no longer afraid; dull resignation had taken over. For her, I thought, the money was the only thing that had ever mattered.

Knuckles rapped on the door. She opened it without any hesitation, and he blew in talking fast the way he did when he was keyed up. "Oh, baby, baby, we did it, we pulled it off," and he grabbed her and started to pull her against him. That was when he saw me.

"Hello, Cohalan," I said.

He went **rigid** for three or four seconds, his eyes popped wide, then disentangled himself from the woman and stood gawping at me. His mouth worked but nothing came out. Manic as hell in his office, all nerves and talking a blue streak, but now he was speechless. Lies were easy for him; the truth would have to be dragged out.

I told him to close the door. He did it, automatically, and turned snarling on Annette Byers. "You let him follow you home!"

"I didn't," she said. "He already knew about me. He knows everything."

"No, you're lying . . ."

"You were so goddamn smart, you had it all figured out. You didn't fool him for a minute."

"Shut up." His eyes shifted to me. "Don't listen to her. She's the one who's been blackmailing me—"

"Knock it off, Cohalan," I said. "Nobody's been blackmailing you. You're the shakedown artist here, you and Annette—a fancy little scheme to get your wife's money. You couldn't just grab the whole bundle from her, and you couldn't get any of it by divorcing her because a spouse's inheritance isn't community property in this state. So you cooked up the phony blackmail scam. What were the two of you planning to do with the full hundred thousand? Run off somewhere together? Buy a load of crank for resale, try for an even bigger score?"

"You see?" Annette Byers said bitterly. "You see, smart guy? He knows everything."

Cohalan shook his head. He'd gotten over his initial shock; now he looked stricken, and his nerves were acting up again. His hands had begun repeating that scoop-shovel trick at his sides. "You believed me, I know you did."

"Wrong," I said. "I didn't believe you. I'm a better actor than you, is all. Your story didn't sound right from the first. Too elaborate, full of improbabilities. Fifty thousand is too big a blackmail bite for any crime short of homicide, and you swore to me—your wife too—you weren't guilty of a major felony. Blackmailers seldom work in big bites anyway. They bleed their victims slow and steady, in small bites, to keep them from throwing the hook. We just didn't believe it, either of us."

"We? Jesus, you mean . . . you and Carolyn . . . ?"

"That's right. Your wife's my client, Cohalan, not you—that's why I never asked you for a retainer. She showed up at my office right after you did the first time; if she hadn't I'd probably have gone to her. She's been suspicious all along, but she gave you the benefit of the doubt until you hit her with the fifty-thousand dollar sum. She figured you might be having an affair, too, and it didn't take me long to find out about Annette. You never had any idea you were being followed, did you? Once I knew about her, it was easy enough to put the rest of it together, including the funny business with the money drop tonight. And here we are."

"Damn you," he said, but there was no heat in the words. "You and that frigid bitch both."

He wasn't talking about Annette Byers, but she took the opportunity to dig into him again. "Smart guy. Big genius. I told you to just take the money and we'd run with it, didn't I?"

"Shut up."

"Don't tell me to shut up, you son of—"

"Don't say it. I'll slap you silly if you say it."

"You won't slap anybody," I said. "Not as long as I'm around."

He wiped his mouth on the sleeve of his jacket. "What're you going to do?"

"What do you think I'm going to do?"

"You can't go to the police. You don't have any proof, it's your word against ours."

"Wrong again." I showed him the voice-activated recorder I'd had hidden in my pocket all evening. High-tech, state-of-the-art equipment, courtesy of George Agonistes, fellow PI and electronics expert. "Everything that was said in your office and in this room tonight is on here. I've also got the cassette tape Annette played when she called earlier. Voice prints will prove the muffled voice on it is yours, that you were talking to yourself on the phone, giving yourself orders and directions. If your wife wants to press charges, she'll have more than enough evidence to put the two of you away."

"She won't press charges," he said. "Not Carolyn."

"Maybe not, if you return the rest of her money. What you and baby here haven't already blown."

He sleeved his mouth again. "I suppose you intend to take the briefcase straight to her."

"You suppose right."

"I could stop you," he said, as if he were trying to convince himself. "I'm as big as you, younger—I could take it away from you."

I repocketed the recorder. I could have showed him the .38, but I grinned at him instead. "Go ahead and try. Or else move away from the door. You've got five seconds to make up your mind."

He moved in three, as I started toward him. Sideways,

clear of both me and the door. Annette Byers let out a sharp, scornful laugh, and he whirled on her—somebody his own size to face off against. "Shut your stupid mouth!" he yelled at her.

"Shut yours, big man. You and your brilliant ideas."

"Goddamn you . . ."

I went out and closed the door against their vicious, whining voices.

Outside the fog had thickened to a near drizzle, slicking the pavement and turning the lines of parked cars along both curbs into two-dimensional black shapes. Parking was at such a premium in this neighborhood there was now a car, dark and silent, double-parked across the street. I walked quickly to California. Nobody, police included, had bothered my wheels in the bus zone. I locked the briefcase in the trunk, let myself inside. A quick call to Carolyn Cohalan to let her know I was coming, a short ride out to her house by the zoo to deliver the fifty thousand, and I'd be finished for the night.

Only she didn't answer her phone.

Funny. When I'd called her earlier from the park, she'd said she would wait for my next call. No reason for her to leave the house in the interim. Unless—

Christ!

I heaved out of the car and ran back down Locust Street. The darkened vehicle was still double-parked across from Annette Byers' building. I swung into the foyer, jammed my finger against the bell button for 2-C and left it there. No response. I rattled the door—latched tight—and then began jabbing buttons on all the other mailboxes. The intercom crackled; somebody's voice said, "Who the hell is that?" I said, "Police emergency, buzz me in." Nothing, nothing, and then finally the door release sounded; I hit the door hard and lunged into the lobby.

I was at the foot of the stairs when the first shot echoed from above. Two more in swift succession, a fourth as I was pounding up to the second floor landing.

Querulous voices, the sound of a door banging open somewhere, and I was at 2-C. The door there was shut but not latched; I kicked it open, hanging back with the .38 in my hand for self-protection. But there was no need. It was over by then. Too late and all over.

All three of them were on the floor. Cohalan on his back next to the couch, blood obscuring his face, not moving. Annette Byers sprawled bloody and moaning by the dinette table. And Carolyn Cohalan sitting with her back against a wall, a long-barreled .22 on the carpet nearby, weeping in deep broken sobs.

I leaned hard on the doorjamb, the stink of cordite in my nostrils, my throat full of bile. Telling myself it was not my fault, there was no way I could have known it wasn't the money but paying them back that mattered to her—the big payoff, the biggest bite there is. Telling myself I could've done nothing to prevent this, and remembering what I'd been thinking in the car earlier, about how I lived for cases like this, how I liked this one a whole lot . . .